MACHINES OF CONSENT

A LESBIAN TRANSFEMME CYBERPUNK NOVEL

SOPHIA TURNER

Edited by: Aurora Foo
Cover art by: Emma Martello
Cover design by: Aurora Foo
Book design by: Sophia Turner

First paperback edition published 2025.

ISBN: 978-1-7638637-2-9

To all the dolls who hold each other and to all the dolls who need to be held

A full list of content warnings are available on the Transistance Press website.

"FUCK!"

The shock had caught Jess — newly Dr. Jess Stockton in formal settings — unaware. Luckily, it hadn't appeared to damage the main board. Her hand, however, still stung.

"Those are not the sparks we were hoping for," Beth replied. Dr. Catalan was no stranger to the odd electronics mishap in the lab, but she wasn't above giving her friend and research partner a good ribbing. They'd been working together for years, and she quietly hoped for years to come.

Between the two women, they held three PhDs and more than a handful of research awards. Jess' own bona fides included a doctorate they had to specially name based on how exceedingly cutting edge her thesis was: bioneurocomputation. The immediate expert of a nascent field, a darling of academia, and quickly the hot item in the expensive field of corporate research.

Beth smiled at her, handing her a translucent shield meant to slip over the front of the device. "Shall we? I think I can get it down to about half the size of the research model. If this works, we might have something."

"What do you mean *if this works?*" Jess teased, though the

tension showed clearly. "Let's do this before I start having doubts and feel like I need to run all the tests again."

Without a word, Beth clicked a translucent shield on her own version of the same device. Using a strap, she attached the device around her neck, letting it rest against her collarbone. She could feel the buzz of the device automatically starting up, perhaps a bit too tingly for most people. She'd have to fix that, too.

"Let's start simple. Say something nice." Beth's voice cooled into a professional tone but kept the crackle of the woman behind it.

Jess slipped on her own device and turned to her friend and coworker. "Close your eyes. Good. Speaking of your eyes — your eyes are like the moon over a still lake. A reflection of your calm soul."

"Wow, that was cheesy," Beth said, but kept her eyes closed. Jess watched as the light in the device around her coworker's neck stirred to life. The readout, a colour shown in the cover of the device — complete with a unique pattern for each colour — told of the general state of the wearer. Specifically, their level of comfort in what was happening and who was speaking.

Beth's device glowed a blue, with a matching pattern. Friendliness.

"How do you feel?" Jess asked, making sure her coworker's eyes stayed closed.

"Just thinking about how nice it is to be friends and working on this project together." Beth opened her eyes and smiled when she saw the look of success on Jess' face. After years of working together, that telltale grin said a thousand words. "That worked, shall we try something negative?"

Jess just nodded and then steadied herself and shut her eyes.

"I should call up my ex and see if I can line up something for tonight," Beth said, the warmth gone from her voice as she stared hard at her friend.

Jess' device swirled into a life of its own, a mix of red and green seemingly wrestling without end. Anger. Jealousy. Bordering on nauseous rage.

"Hey sorry, sorry." Beth jumped to action, arms around Jess in a hold that wouldn't let her go until she knew she was okay. "We had to try it. I promise that was just a test. Promise."

Once Beth felt comfortable letting go, she added, "Looks like it worked. Shall we try a final test?"

Jess nodded, then shut her eyes.

"Oh, I think you'll want to leave your eyes open for this one," Beth added.

Jess did as she suggested, and soon her eyes grew large as Beth reached and unhooked her lab coat, letting it fall open. Beth smiled as she eyed the purple glow at Jess' neck.

"I think yours is working, too," Jess said, her eyes darting between her friend's bare skin and the device at her neck.

Beth looked down and caught the purple glow of her own device. "Well, then. I guess we should think of a name. But first, we should see how well these work in more intense situations..."

JESS

Jess lowered her glass and marvelled at how her dinner companion's hair framed her face so perfectly. Around her neck, worn tightly to match her outfit, was a choker with a large gem in the middle. A very special gem.

A Bonobo Device.

The wonder of modern technology that had saved friendship and relationship alike. And, honestly, probably hurt a few. All told, though, it had been a boon.

Its faint colour, a warm amber, and a lovely set of gyrating shapes told Jess all she needed to know about how the evening was going. Amber meant embrace. Engage. Nuzzle. This was a comfortable place to be, and if that's how it stayed for the evening, Jess would be content.

Jess didn't have to look at her own Bonobo. Its purple and corresponding pattern shone proudly for all to see. People just got used to seeing "I want to fuck you" glow in the jewel-shaped device. No one was bothered. No one was threatened. Her dinner companion was pleasant conversation and definitely Jess' type. If she wanted the same thing, her Bonobo would change to match.

Jess was more than happy to engage and later, perhaps, to embrace.

She thought idly of the clinical trials of this device she ran before its widespread use. How many men were shocked to find their dinner companions didn't secretly want to bang them. Such horror. The devices were broken. Surely, they were misreporting the results! No hun, she's just not into you.

What she felt especially proud of was how much the Bonobo cut down on assaults. Pushing someone beyond the allowance shown in the colour was now against the law. The more above the line, the higher the punishment. With most folks paying for the add-on response service, her yearly bonuses got noticeably larger, too.

Everyone wanted one. Dating apps started requiring them. Fake ones appeared on the market, so the real ones had to learn how to detect fake ones and warn the owner.

A silly tech cat and mouse game that Jess was more than happy to keep playing so that they could stay on top. She kept secret that she had anything to do with its development. It just wouldn't do. She didn't want to be famous like past tech innovators. She wanted to meet people and never see a glimpse of anything other than simple interest or disinterest. Ironic, she knew.

Her companion smiled at her and asked about dessert.

"Dessert sounds lovely," Jess said. "If you like, I have some of the most decadent chocolate cake in the city back at my apartment."

Jess had a few apartments. Easier to seem normal that way, rather than having one large mansion.

"I'd like that."

Jess didn't let herself smile at the hint of purple that flecked the steady amber. *Good girl,* she thought quietly to herself. She likes being spoiled. We can work with that.

"Shall we?" With that, the two of them paid and exited.

———

"Fuck. Fuck. Fuck. Fuck." This girl should have been a drummer. Her rhythm was impeccable. Jess' hand kept steady time with it as she drove the girl higher.

The chocolate sauce was a risk, though it seemed to have paid off splendidly. Her companion's glowing violet gem was almost unnecessary when taken with the hot flushing of her face. Oh, and Jess's fingers buried inside her.

Still, she kept a watch on it. Keeping her happy and open meant this stayed legal. Which is precisely what Jess wanted to do.

Plus, consent was fucking sexy.

She leaned in and licked more chocolate off her companion's nipples. The combo of the sweet sauce with the woman under her mewing was dizzying. She fought the urge to pump her harder and drive her over the edge, instead opting to keep the slow pace and let things drag out longer.

She had too much chocolate on her to attempt to go down on her companion while fingering her. Jess wasn't going to spoil the evening like that.

But it did give her an idea.

"Would you mind if we changed positions?" Jess watched her, and her jewel, as she slowed her hand.

"You've got something else in mind you'd like to try?"

Jess smiled. "I thought you might like to dine on honey while I finished cleaning you off."

"Oh fuck, yes."

Jess' smile widened. She gently pulled herself out and then straddled her companion's face. On a whim, she massaged the chocolate-smeared breasts below her. The sensation of tasting vagina while being food massaged must have been too much for her. Jess watched her companion finger fuck herself furiously as her tongue dove deeper. It was an impressively long tongue, and Jess was happy to ride it. Her companion finished in a fever of moans that sent vibrations up into Jess.

She slowly eased herself off her companion and smiled down at her. "Don't worry, you don't have to finish me. I enjoyed the show."

She watched the dark purple of the jewel fade at her comment.

"You sure? I'm happy to try if you have time." It was a sweet offer. Jess took a few seconds to think it over.

"I appreciate it, but I have an early day tomorrow. I should probably get some rest."

That was mostly true. True enough it didn't feel like a lie.

Her chocolate layered companion washed off in the shower and then excused herself politely. Jess let her go without any resistance. It was just a one-time thing. Sadly, all too often, people she met were just one-time things.

———

Last night's reverie felt like a hangover the next morning. She looked up and down at her notes for the next four test subjects. Each one exhibited some surprise in the data. Normally, her assistant would oversee the retesting, but today she felt like getting her hands dirty.

In something other than chocolate sauce.

The first two retests were nothing out of the ordinary. They had a glitch in their data, but it couldn't be reproduced. Maybe they had sneezed or had an inspired understanding of jazz while getting tested the first time. Who knows? It didn't matter.

The third test subject walked in, and Jess almost dropped

her tablet. She didn't normally have this kind of reaction to women.

But here was this perfect pixie cut, girl-next-door who was likely none the wiser of the effect she was having on Jess, who, in an effort not to contaminate the test data, was not wearing her jewel. She thanked her lucky stars she was not.

The subject's name was listed as "Roh", no last name.

"Hi Roh, I'm Jess. I'll be helping run your retest today. It says here that you have no reactions with the Bonobo Device. Have you by chance had a brain injury that might impede the device?"

Roh turned to at her. Her face looked slightly like a lost puppy, like she was from a different era and had been surprised one day to awaken in this one.

"Not to my knowledge."

Jess looked back to her tablet. "Are you, to your knowledge, part of an alien race?"

That one gave Roh a small smirk. Her little movement sent a drop of warmth into Jess' belly. Then, she shook her head. "Not to my knowledge."

"Did you tamper with, damage, or disable the Bonobo Device during the test?"

She simply shook her head no in response.

"I'm sorry, I'll need a verbal response."

"No."

She was hiding something, but Jess couldn't decipher what. Not yet. She felt her brain prickle at the possibility of cracking this woman open and learning her secrets.

Jess studied Roh's face as long as felt reasonable, but it yielded nothing.

"Then, with that, it's time to re-run the test. We'll do the same steps as before, only this time we have two observers: myself and Dr. Catalan over there behind the glass. If you have any questions, we can pause the test to answer them, but as this is your second time, I don't imagine we'll have any trouble."

Roh just nodded and stepped up to the table. Jess fitted the lab Bonobo Device around her neck.

"We'll show you a set of pictures on the screen in front of you. Just relax and watch them go by. Your body should do the rest. We'll be recording you during this test. I'll begin the recording now."

Jess reached over and hit the button to begin the recording, then a second button to begin the test video playing on the terminal in front of Roh. She quietly watched Roh as each image showed on the monitor. Something about her face that Jess couldn't quite place felt warm and alluring, though she admitted that Roh herself felt a bit prickly.

Jess checked the device. Sure enough, after it had time to sync itself with Roh it started sending data back to her tablet. She could see the responses, but she just couldn't believe them. Roh was managing to suppress the device's ability to read her mood, her state of desire and acceptance. She had readings, sure, but it was almost as if values of her pulse, sweat, blood pressure, blood cortisol levels, etc were all set by a computer meant to scramble the device. No human would be able to produce values like that.

Jess bit back the urge to ask her how she was doing this. Surely, she had a microchip buried under her skin that was giving false data.

Once the test had run, Jess raised her hand at the elbow.

"As we have time, I'd like to re-run that test. Would you consent to sticking around a bit longer?"

Roh nodded. "I'm getting paid for the hour either way, so I'm happy to."

Jess called in the lab rats, who pulled up a full machine on wheels, completely with enough suction cuts it made the device look like it had tentacles. They expertly placed the cups around Roh's body. Jess tried her best to ignore the gentle swell of Roh's breasts as they finished.

"This machine should help us make sure that the readings the Bonobo Device line up with readings from other parts of your body. Generally, this isn't necessary, but the human body can be a strange, fickle thing."

She restarted the tests, making sure the camera was on.

She stared at her tablet this time. EKG, blood readings, all of them were there. They all matched the Bonobo Device to within an acceptable error margin. Jess gawked. It simply wasn't possible.

As expected, the Bonobo Device could not function with these kinds of conflicting readings. The body worked in harmony, in a very understandable concert of ups and downs. Roh, however, looked like every heartbeat, every amount of cortisol, even every breath was random. Almost completely random. With that kind of chaos, the Bonobo Device was useless.

As the test wound down, Jess set the tablet to the side. "How are you feeling, Roh?"

Roh shrugged. "I feel fine."

"May I touch your arm?" Jess asked without thinking about it. At this point, she wanted to reach out and confirm Roh was actually flesh and blood.

Without a word, Roh stepped around the table and offered her arm to Jess. Up close, Jess could really appreciate just how fit Roh was. She didn't have the body of a weightlifter. More like a gymnast. Square shoulders and muscular, lean arms. The effect was immediate. Jess' cheeks burned as blood rushed to them. Jess forced her gaze up, only to find Roh already looking into her eyes.

The eye contact unsettled Jess, but she made herself focus

and gently take Roh's arm. She felt for her pulse. The rhythm was there, though inhuman. Where one would expect a ba-BUM, she had a baaah-buh-BUM. Not human, but close.

"Do you feel any chest pains? Dizziness?"

Roh shook her head.

Without much thought, Jess slid her hands down to Roh's hand and felt it for a moment. It was warm. Human. Natural. And yet...

She let go.

"Thank you for coming in. Just as before, reception will have your payment waiting for you. If we need for you to come in again for additional tests, are you available?"

Roh nodded, her eyes still locked onto Jess'. "As long as there is payment, I'm happy to let you poke me." With that, she broke eye contact and walked past Jess out the door to the lab.

Jess turned to the observation window. "Did you see that?"

The observation speaker clicked on, and soon the air was filled with Dr. Beth Catalan's warm voice. "Are you asking me as a colleague or as a friend?" Beth was never one to shy away from a good tease.

Jess' mouth went dry. She picked up the tablet.

"Let's start with the data first," she said, chasing the few words with a large drink of coffee. It was tepid, and it wasn't even that great to begin with. Still, anything was welcome.

Beth's voice again came over the intercom. "I think she lied about being an alien."

They shared a laugh, but it felt true in some way. Roh definitely didn't read like a human. At least, not like any human she'd ever met.

2

CHICKEN AND CHIPS

ROH

Roh tightened her laces and relaxed at the thought of being less broke than she was an hour ago. She took off at an easy pace toward the central city district.

The lab lady this time was cute in a kind of nerdy way. Hair pinned back and that ridiculous lab coat. She seemed about Roh's height when she wasn't fussing and fidgeting. She also, apparently, was very gay. The way she blushed on eye contact and couldn't take her eyes off her. The way she wanted to accidentally hold hands at the end of the test. Roh smiled at herself. It's nice her charms had an effect. Who knew, maybe they'd run into each other again at some point.

She knew better than to trust those scientist types, though. It's all fun and games until you wake up in some kind of horrible teleporter accident. You're screaming. You have the wings of a grasshopper. It's a whole thing.

Roh lived her life in a far more predictable way. If not predictable, then at least the surprises were less grasshoppery in nature.

She let her legs find an easy pace as she banished the horrible image from her mind. With that, she took in her surroundings. This city. She knew it like the back of her hand. Every turn. Every alley. The skyscrapers with their maze of bridges, dozens of stories off the ground. The underground with its dark network of turns and access ways. Every blaring billboard trying to get attention. She even knew some of the suburbs that pushed out into the wastes, though she rarely needed to visit them for her work.

She wasn't particularly proud of the path she had to take to get here, but she was fiercely proud of the woman she'd become. A fighter. A survivor.

She tapped the bud on the inside of her ear and let it choose some electronic track that matched her stride rhythm. As if on cue, her phone buzzed. A delivery — and nearby at that. Good. She'd make a bit more money today to go with being a lab rat. She might even be able to splash out a bit for dinner.

She watched as cars zipped past her, finding her spot.

The city could also be a dangerous place. Folks tended to stick to the areas they knew, but there were always corners to be afraid of in this city. Cesspools that would drag you down and never let you out. She'd managed to avoid them all. Sure, she did jobs. Everyone who spent time on the street had done jobs. She had a rap sheet and a resume, and to some folks those were one and the same.

At the end of the day, it was the basics: food, shelter, and making the next day a little easier than the last. That was it. The rest was stress and perhaps some occasional gravy.

She slowed her pace as she noticed someone subtly motioning for her out of the corner of her eye. Geoff the Barber was his name. On a good day he was merely gruff. Roh crossed her fingers and hoped for a good day. She reached up and clicked her music off.

"You look like you need some chicken and chips. Boss said to keep your eyes up."

Roh stared at him but didn't respond immediately. A dangerous package, then. Don't drop it and don't get caught. She gave him a quick nod, carefully lifted the package from his arms and turned, her mind filling with possible routes. Her destination was a good thirty minutes away if she could run straight to it.

She could chance the open for a bit, until she felt someone following her. It would save time, but it was a risk.

Her senses tuned. She knew better than to block out the city. It would speak to her and keep her safe if she used her training and listened.

Sure enough. Only a couple of minutes after leaving Geoff, she felt a tingle at the back of her neck. Not daring to turn around, she kept forward and visualised the city in her mind. There was a manhole a block away that would drop her into the upper sewers. The sewers would take longer, and if they knew them as well as she did, they could box her in. There were multiple businesses she could enter as a courier and get up into the upper-ways. Calculating the risks, she decided on a third option.

She picked up her pace and cut towards a construction site of a development complex that had stalled out for lack of funds. The sound of a car turning too sharply behind her told her all she needed to know. She took off, hitting the fence at full speed, catapulting over it with the taut power of her momentum and her free hand. She made sure to land softly enough to keep the package undisturbed.

Ramp, up, stairs right, then to the roof. She'd only used this building once before, but it was exactly as she remembered. Soon, she'd gained the roof and was looking out at the street and neighbouring buildings. She ran along the joists and aimed her body towards the next roof, a multi-tiered tenant building. From there, a swift climb up a ladder, and a cross along a metal-covered skybridge.

She listened as she crossed. It didn't sound like she'd been spotted. Just another day as a courier.

She flowed around the buildings as long as she could and finally dropped down behind a large building a few blocks later. They'd be looking for her, but there were too many alleys to search them all.

———

The route was slow but thankfully as safe as she hoped. Over an hour later, and Roh popped up near one of the best chicken shops in town. A bright, yet otherwise unassuming restaurant on the ground floor of an old building in an old section of town. Rather than go to the front, she went around back.

The backdoor was ajar.

She opened it and peeked in. "Got anything good?" One of the workers peeled around the corner and walked up to her.

She pulled out her bundle and handed it to him. He disappeared and returned carrying something. He handed her the bundle, which smelled suspiciously like a deluxe chicken and chips with extra chicken salt.

She salivated.

"Boss thought you might want some dinner."

Her phone buzzed, but she didn't check it. For all their fuckery, doing jobs paid promptly.

She thanked him and walked around into the front entrance of the shop and sat at one of the empty tables in front of the window. She ate and absent-mindedly watched as the volume of salarymen passing the window grew. By the time she'd finished, the sky had started to dim.

She stayed off the major streets and lazily made her way to her apartment. Two payoffs in a day? Worth it. And she got a free lunch/dinner. She could cut out early and relax on the couch.

———

Roh's front door swung open with the same familiarity it always did, followed by the even more familiar mewing of her favourite life-form in the whole world.

"Hi, Max."

She reached down to lavish him with some good head scritches.

"Holding down the fort?"

Max trotted in front of her, mewing as he went.

"I thought so. Reminding me where the good stuff is?"

Max's mewing got more insistent.

"I thought so."

Roh locked the door behind her and followed her feline friend to the kitchen, throwing her keys in the dish on the way.

"Hey buddy, you would never guess what I had for lunch today."

Max's mewing turned quizzical but stayed insistent.

"Yeah, that's a good guess." She reached up in the cupboard and got out the plastic bin of dry cat food, pouring Max a healthy serving in his bowl. "There you go buddy." She returned the bin to the cabinet and shut the door, then slid down to be with Max on the kitchen floor.

She closed her eyes and mentally counted off the money in her account. She needed to do at least two more jobs before she could relax for the week. There were three days. It should be doable. Maybe that lab lady would call her up and ask for more... assistance.

She smiled as she felt Max take over her lap. "Hey good sir. Enjoy your meal?"

Methodically, she let her hands scritch him in all his favourite places. When her hands got to where his collar would be, she froze.

She opened her eyes and looked at him. "Max, buddy, where's your collar? You know I love you but that's not something I thought you could take off. As cute as you are, you don't have thumbs."

She gently moved him off her so she could stand. She pulled out her phone and clicked on her tracking app, only to find the collar was not in her apartment.

"Oh, fuck."

3

ILLEGAL AND HOT

JESS

"Interesting day." Beth opened her driver-side door and got in. She adjusted the Bonobo at her throat and then checked herself in the rearview mirror.

Jess got in on the passenger side. "Uh huh" was all she was able to manage.

Beth turned to her long-time friend and smiled before she started the car. "You want to talk about it?"

Then, Beth took a second look before she put the car in reverse. Jess' Bonobo Device was cycling through a variety of colours. Already, she was lost in her own world.

"Is it the readings or the girl?" Beth pulled the car out and headed toward their favourite restaurant.

"Doesn't make sense." It wasn't really a full sentence. Beth was used to it. Sometimes, it meant a breakthrough was about to happen. More times than not, though, she was just unanchored in a sea of thought with no destination. On bad days, it could take hours for her to come back out again.

"I agree. Should we try some different tests?" Beth chanced a glance over at her passenger, then back to the road.

Nothing.

Jess was quiet the rest of the way. Once they were seated at the restaurant, Jess turned to Beth, locking eyes as she brandished her fork in the air. "Who is she? What is she?"

Beth laughed, though she leaned back defensively. "A woman, I'd guess. A human, possibly." She chuckled again, though she was studying Jess for a reaction. Jess didn't seem like she'd heard a word.

Beth leaned in, and in a low whisper said, "Jess, you look like you need a good milking."

That did it. Water shot out of her mouth across the table. Red-faced, Jess turned back to her friend, her Bonobo taking on distinctive purple stripes.

"Oh my god, fuck you."

"Welcome back," Beth smiled, happily dabbing at the spray that hit her with a napkin. "Where have you been?"

"Sorry," she said, dabbing her mouth with her own napkin. "I just can't get her out of my head."

"Test subject #3 from today?"

Jess nodded.

"Do you think she's hot?"

Jess' blush grew deeper. "That might be adding to my fascination, yes. But I'm a scientist first and foremost."

Beth shook her head. "No, my dear friend, you're a woman first and foremost. With needs, I might add. Admittedly, that does complicate the science a bit."

Jess nodded. "Just a little bit." She flagged down the waiter for another glass of water, apologising at the mess with a few words, and then turned back to Beth.

Beth inhaled sharply, then looked to the ceiling in her customary position of summoning the great sciences muses. "What do we know? We know she had some kind of arrhythmia unlike any we've ever seen. Chemically, her body responds more like a sports car to stress and stimulus, as opposed to the sedans the rest of us drive around." Beth watched as Jess' Bonobo took on a deeper purple. "Really? That's what did it? Thinking of her like a sports car, and now you want to ride her?"

They shared a chuckle. Jess looked for her fork and poked at her food. "Twelve years and we've never seen anything like this."

"Don't remind me." Beth snorted. "I don't know how we managed those first few years. The thought of sleeping in a blanket on the floor, getting up every couple hours to check on test results. Thirty-hour shifts. The very idea makes me want to call my chiro." Jess chewed on her broccoli, its light seasoning a pleasant offset to the rest of the plate, and the reserve of water she'd put there moments earlier.

They ate for a few moments in silence.

Beth whispered, only loud enough for Jess to hear. "I think she's genetically modified. That's the only thing that makes sense."

Jess slowed her chewing, swallowed, and put down her fork. "That... would be highly illegal."

"But not impossible."

Jess nodded. "But not impossible." She thought for a moment, and then, her face matched her resolve. "I'm not going to report it, either. We don't know the story. We only have evidence of the possibility, but not evidence of the deed. It's not our battle to fight. I'll be honest, even if it was..."

Beth shook her head. "Agreed, even if it was, that's not something we want to get mixed up with. Then, we shelve it? Write her up as an anomaly in the data and drop her in the aggregate like the outlier she is? It shouldn't impact our development. How's that sound?"

Jess had that far-away look in her eyes again.

"You're not going to drop her, are you?"

"What? No. I mean, yes, we should just treat her as an outlier and move on. No need to call her back into the office."

Beth chuckled. "Why does your face tell me something different than what your mouth is telling me?"

"Look, just because I want to fuck her doesn't mean I'll bring her back to the lab to jeopardise what we're doing. I can keep my libido in check, at least that much."

"Good, because I'm in the mood for donuts. My turn to pay, by the way."

———

The two of them laughed over their desserts in their favourite donut shop in the area. Business was rather slow, but even if it wasn't, Ariel — the shop's owner — always made time to stick her head in their conversations, and they happily took her opinion and ran with it.

"...but that's easily the best rock band of all time," Ariel said, ringing up a customer and walking back over to where they were sitting at the bar.

Jess pointed her fork. "Sure, greatest rock band of all time. You should be glad rock is dead so you can make that claim."

Ariel groaned and polished one of the glasses. "My case rests."

It was always like this, which is why going for donuts after dinner was a regular habit. Neither of them drank much, maybe the occasional glass of wine over dinner, so this became their stand-in for the pub life. Well worth it, they often agreed.

Jess finished licking the sugar off her fingers, knowing in the back of her mind she would never let propriety take over. The better demon always seemed to win the day.

"Look who just came in." Beth's voice was in a hush, and it filled Jess with curiosity.

Standing in the doorway was the likely-genetically-modified test subject #3, the very same one less than an hour earlier she tried to swear off.

"You're joking."

BAD NEWS OVER CEVICHE

ROH

Roh pushed her way into the donut shop. She knew that asshole Benjar was likely going to be here at this time of day. His was a hard face to forget. All the time they spent together in the early days to teach her the art of the messenger. How to run. How to get out of tight situations. Years of it. In that time, she got to learn his ins and outs. He had habits. This was one of his more legal ones.

The first thing that caught her eye wasn't Benjar. It was the woman eye-fucking her from her seat at the counter, her Bonobo Device instantly switching to purple when the woman saw her walk in.

She looked familiar, but Roh had other priorities.

She spotted him.

Roh beelined to his seat, pinched his shoulder, and leaned in. "Benjy! We need to talk."

"Have a seat, Roh. I haven't finished, yet." He motioned to the empty bench with a meaty finger covered in chocolate.

Roh obliged.

"You look like you had half a mind to create a scene, eh? Throw me out on my face. Would have been a pretty sight.

Show the one who taught you how to survive on the streets who's really boss? Maybe you're trying to impress that hottie at the bar?"

"Fuck you, Benjar." Roh sighed.

Benjar raised his hands. "Look, I'm not here to convince you to behave, but it's in your best interest to do so. I trust you have a good reason for the intrusion. Not that, uh, I mind the company." He fed himself a careful bite, then slowly wiped the mess from his lips with a practised flip of his serviette. "Whatever you think is happening might not be happening how you think it's happening."

"What?" Roh cursed herself for being at her absolute most eloquent.

"Someone did you wrong, eh? Someone did you dirty, and you think it's gotta be Benjar. Gotta be that man who always has it out for me. Always wants to get one-up on me. You know the street, kid. It's not like bad blood runs forever. Eventually, the rain washes it down in the gutters. People move on." He leaned back and stretched his arms across the bench.

He nodded to himself as if agreeing with a thought that came to him. "I'm going to do you a favour. But first you're going to do me one. See, you interrupted my quiet time. My quiet place. This is where I meditate over my happy plates of goodness. But you interrupted my meditation. I wasn't finished, kid. You know what they say about interrupting meditation before you finish."

Roh had no idea what they said, but she kept her mouth shut.

"Go get me something. Crème-filled, cake, whatever. Get something good. Then I'll tell ya what you want to know."

Roh locked eyes with him as if to ask '*are you fucking serious?*'. He didn't budge, so she pushed herself off the bench and walked up to the counter.

That woman was still there. She spun around as Roh approached the bar. No wonder she looked familiar, she looked like that woman from the lab. She *was* that woman from the lab.

Roh motioned to the proprietor. "Can I get two of the cookies and crème? Please?" She fished her phone out of her front pocket. She let the woman staring holes into the side of her face get a good look.

Then, curiosity hit her. She slowly turned as the donuts slid across the counter. Her features were actually quite striking when she wasn't lit with lab lights. Her hair down, it framed her face well, which had a pleasant roundness to it. Roh had to admit her eyes were more expressive than the device around her neck. She was hungry, yes. But she was also very lonely.

Something Roh knew all too well herself.

Roh felt a chill run up her spine. She almost opened her mouth when she heard the proprietor. She grabbed the donuts and swiped her card.

As she spun around, a single syllable escaped her lips. "Fuck." In that time, Benjar had split.

"Did your date run out on you?" It was the woman. Roh couldn't remember her name, though she was finding she wished she could. "At least he has good taste in dessert. And women."

Roh gave a half cough. "He thinks he's real fucking funny."

"Who, your date?" the woman asked.

Roh shook her head. "He was most definitely not my date."

The woman chuckled. "You are a bit out of his league."

Roh turned to her. This woman was relentless. "What about you? You go after many of the lab rats you meet in your line of work?"

"Roh, would it surprise you if I told you the answer was

'no'?" The woman slid a bill across the table that had to be far more than enough to cover the food she and her friend had eaten.

Roh paused. The woman remembered her name. She felt one-upped.

"Look, I'm not sure exactly what to say," Roh admitted. "But, I've got to track that man down. He owes me more than two donuts." Almost as an offhanded thought, she added. "If you're that interested, you know where to find me."

She left the donuts on the counter, apologised to the proprietor, and headed out the door.

Once in the parking lot, Roh spun around looking for any car she recognised, but he was long gone. It was more than likely he'd been called off rather than he'd run off. He was a bit too powerful to fear anything from Roh, and she knew that. At most, she could give him a good scare.

Her phone buzzed. Pulling it out of her pocket, she let herself smile. At least he was polite enough to apologise in his own way.

"I owe you a donut, kid. Tonight, have some ceviche on me."

He'd invited her to the den. Where she was sure she didn't want to be. But if she wanted answers, there weren't many options.

She shook her head. More fish seemed to be on the menu.

———

Roh looked around at the den.

She always sized up everyone anywhere she went. Habit. Benjar alone, Roh knew she could handle. But the den? The den was full of enough people with a chip and a dream that they'd do anything to prove themselves to the higher ups. If she was unlucky, she'd be their ticket to a promotion. Maybe because she sneezed wrong and caught the boss's new suit in the blast. It could be anything.

The only protection she had was her wits. Even her agility wouldn't give her much advantage in the den's centrepiece, a bar that used fresh, locally sourced ingredients regularly. She had to admit, it tasted good. But the food made her feel dirty. Kept. Owned. It reminded her of her stupid, younger years.

Once the doors closed, that was it. They liked to do things the old way. Once you were in, you were in, until they told you that you could leave. She would never call them mobsters, at least not to their face. But, if the shoe fit...

Benjar, true to his word, sat at a table just off to the right. Roh took a breath and stepped into the room.

"Roh, come on over, you'll never believe what they have on the menu tonight."

Me, probably, Roh thought.

She slid in across from him, having no small amount of déjà vu. "You owe me dessert, Benjy." She looked around, feeling more than a little unsteady.

"Relax. Here, I'll get you the special. You'll love it."

She turned to face him. "You know something."

He nodded. "I know many somethings. I suspect some of them you want to know for yourself." He pointed to her and then unfolded his serviette into his lap. He waved a hand and the waiter took his order and disappeared quietly. "Some of them are going to cost ya. More than a few donuts, mind."

She folded her arms. "Look, there's really only one thing I want to know. Who broke into my house, and why."

He chuckled. "That's two things, but I'll let you count them as one since I'm feeling generous. Look, kid, wait til you see this." As if by magic, the waiter reappeared carrying two large bowls of ceviche with handmade crackers.

"Good, dinner is served." Benjar raised his hands and let the bowl be set down in front of him. "Dig in. Nothing good is ever truly solved on an empty stomach."

Roh couldn't tell if he was stalling or just hungry. There was no fighting either way. She dug into her dinner, which was as fresh and satisfying as she knew it would be.

Finally, after a few minutes, Benjar looked up from his bowl. "You've got yourself a problem."

"With the Bermanns?"

Benjar shook his head. "A bigger problem."

Roh froze.

"Right, kid. That kind of problem. You didn't happen to go to a lab to get tests run that might have found their way into the wrong hands, did you?"

"Fuuuuck." Roh set down her fork, suddenly not hungry.

"You think any lab is secure these days? That wasn't very smart, was it? For a few credits you could have gotten somewhere else. You can always have your old job back. I meant what I said about bad blood being long gone." Benjar happily piled ceviche on a cracker and took a bite, moaning slightly as he chewed. "It's a tough world out there, kid. You're either the fish, or you're the fisherman. Well, fisherwoman."

His concession to her gender was laughable. He couldn't care less what she was if she could produce results.

"Maybe I'll become a vegetarian, so I don't have to pick a side."

Benjar chuckled. "You think the vegetables get much say in who eats them? You better get on top of this one, kid. You're exposed. They found you, know where you live, and you better make a move, or they'll make theirs."

Roh looked up, her forehead folded in thought. "This lab. Do you think they're working with them?"

Benjar shrugged and scooped another handful of fish and

avocado into his mouth. "Look, I gave you what I can tell you for free. Your turn. If you want more, you'll have to work. Either that, or you go find out for yourself. Just watch your back if you do. Your time with me was easy compared to what they'll want."

Roh swallowed her next words and took a breath. "Thanks, Benjy. That's helpful. Now, am I allowed to go?"

"Always kid. Sorry to spoil your appetite."

Always, yeah right. She knew she'd just gotten lucky tonight. She didn't know why she had, but she wasn't about to push her luck further.

Safely outside the den, she looked around. She had another stop to make tonight, and it was going to be considerably harder than the first.

5

WHERE THE ARROWS POINT

JESS

Beth entered the living room wrapped in towels, her cheeks still sporting a healthy glow. Jess looked up at her, neatly surrounded by piles of reports.

"You look ready to dive in," Beth said as she pulled the towel off her head and gave her hair a series of gentle pats.

Beth motioned to a book Jess had pulled out while Beth showered. It was the perfect height to help Jess organise the her research, though she hadn't been paying much attention to which book she'd grabbed. She leaned over and read the spine. It was one of her many books on Buddhism, a topic she couldn't help but look on with some fondness.

"You were so into it, I thought we might lose you. You know, become a nun or something." Beth smiled, her glow steadily beaming.

"Yeah, imagine my face when I tried to say the vows. I miss it, though." Jess' face drew into a thoughtful poise. "Loved the practices. Loved the time to reflect and focus. I still practice a bit, though not nearly as much as I probably should."

Beth chuckled. "You've got other ways to channel your energies these days." She reached over to a stack of her clothes that had magically found themselves folded and ready for her. Jess was always thoughtful in her own ways. Wordlessly, she pulled on her panties and dropped the towel to put on her bra.

Beth motioned at the paperwork while she dressed. "Are we up again?"

Jess tried not to watch her dress out of the corner of her eye, but the temptation was strong. "We are indeed. 'Tis the season for yearly planning. They want to know if we have any big ideas for the next version of the Bonobo."

"Can't they just, you know, enjoy the fruits of our labour for a year and leave us be?"

Jess snorted as she threw up an arm. "But that wouldn't be very capitalist of them."

"Perish the thought." Beth finished pulling on her skirt and shirt and sat nearby. "What are you thinking?"

"You feel up for a rapid-fire?" Jess gestured over to three stacks of papers, neatly sorted. "We can see what sticks."

"Sure, give me one." Beth held out her hands as Jess grabbed a stapled stack of papers and deftly tossed it to her. That sat in silence for a minute as each scanned one of the new research papers that had come out in the last year.

"This one is bullshit." Jess, never one to hold back on an academic assessment, cast aside the one she was reading.

"This one isn't bad, but it'd be impossible for our package size. We're trying to fit into something no larger than half the size of a fist, if not smaller. This would take that plus wires that run around your neck and up to your head."

Jess laughed. "That... doesn't sound very fashionable."

"To say the least."

"Why, what would it do?" Jess turned back to the pile and fished out the next researched paper she'd queued up.

"If we can reproduce the results – and that's the big risk

with these papers – we should be able to get something like coarse-grained emotive reception."

Jess put aside the research paper she was holding. "How the fuck did they pull that off?"

"I'm not entirely sure that they have, we'd have to give it a test. The short of it is that they seem to have engineered the equivalent of a long-range listening device by combining a mesh of wires and some clever interpretation methods from last year's signal processing consortium darlings." Beth continued flipping through it until she got to the results.

"Who would have thought someone would come up with mind-reading in our lifetime," Jess smiled, the idea happily bouncing around in her head.

"Like I said, if it works, it's completely impractical. Got anything else?"

Jess reached down and tossed her the paper she'd set aside.

———

They were about to break for a late dinner when both of their phones buzzed angrily. Instead of checking her messages, Jess pulled up her laptop.

"Fuck."

A break-in. The IT security team had spotted it after it had happened, but not in time to shut it down before they got whatever they were looking for. The team was doing forensics to understand exactly what was copied, but both the potential future IP drives and the research record drives had been accessed. Billions in credits at risk, potentially, if they knew exactly what to grab. The execs were going to want a full report in the morning.

8 am was not far enough away for comfort. She'd give anything for another 24 hours.

Another email popped up on her screen. She reached over and opened it with one hand as her other took the plate Beth offered her. A hot toastie. She'd long ago learned all-nighters were impossible on an empty stomach.

"I figured you'd want that. Do you need me around?" Beth looked ready to stay the night.

"Sadly, this one won't need your engineering skills. They're going to want answers from me, and I have to wait for the sec team to do their job."

Beth leaned over and gave her a light peck on the top of her head. "Try to get at least some sleep," she added, her voice soft.

They both knew she wouldn't.

Jess only vaguely registered the sound of her front door closing as her focus returned to her laptop and the new email.

Just what she was afraid of. The hackers were good. Few, if any, traces were left of where they'd been. They had enough time to get in and clear their tracks on the way out. Best to assume that both the intellectual property records and research records had been compromised. The lawyers would want in on this. Patents would be done where they could be done defensively, corporate recon to find who might be acting like they took the docs, and then wait and see. With luck, they'd meet in negotiations. Someone had just picked a fight, and they were stuck looking for the guilty smile.

"Dammit," Jess swore as she pulled her hand away. Long gone was her toastie, and she'd been chewing on her thumb instead. She made herself calm down and breathe. She was clever. That's what they paid her for. To pay attention to all the details that weren't obvious to anyone else.

Massaging her thumb lightly, she flipped back through the reports on the break-in. She knew she wasn't likely to spot anything. The security team was top-dollar. If there was something they missed in the forensics, she felt confident she'd miss it too. But she liked patterns. She loved patterns. If she could spot something just out of sight and make sense of it, then suddenly taking a second look would be very much worth it.

"Why commercial research records?" She wiped off her fingers with a paper towel. Some things hadn't changed from her school years. "Why not ten other departments that were worth more? We do military research, and they didn't even touch it." She stood up and paced around her apartment. It was shaped just like her old lab room and pacing always seemed to do the trick to help get her brain in gear.

"Why would I break into research records? Wait. What kind of records?"

She clicked back through the early reports and back to the final assessment. Not just any research reports. Research subject reports. People reports.

She hummed to herself and returned to pacing. There was only one reason anyone would want to look at those. It didn't have anything to do with intellectual property.

"Or does it?" she asked her empty apartment.

She went from standing to cross-legged on the floor in one motion, another trick she learned at uni.

She pulled up the records of everyone who had come through the lab in the last week. Visitors, test subjects, experts from some of the other labs on consult. If they were looking for anyone, she thought, it would be recent.

She shivered at the thought of the lab being monitored. It wouldn't surprise her if they were being spied on, but no one wanted to be tailed or watched as they come and go. It's one of the reasons that she kept a relatively low profile. Dalliances aside.

The list, even limited to a week, was pretty substantial. Dozens of people would come in as part of research visits, that plus the retests this week meant a higher volume was coming and going than normal.

Retests.

It could be a visitor, but if they were looking for research subjects specifically, then they'd known someone coming into the lab was explicitly there to be tested on.

"Girl, if this is some elaborate plan to get me to call you back into the lab." She said it as a joke, but as the words hung in the air, they didn't *feel* like a joke. She obsessed over Roh's results for hours, until Beth knocked her out of it. Maybe she wasn't the only one?

The thought of Roh being genetically modified bloomed again in her mind. Was she being tracked? If so, by whom?

She started to pace again. Could she bring Roh back into the office without arousing suspicion? Likely not. If she wasn't being monitored that closely before, she was now. If, that is, she was who they were after.

There was no reason to jump to conclusions that it even was Roh.

And yet...

That same feeling she got when she knew she was close to solving a particularly sticky problem was hounding her. Her instincts, tuned to sniff out the surprise, were alive.

She wasn't just an anomaly.

She was engineered for something. Something this group didn't want other people to know about. But also for something she had yet to perform.

Why else would she still be alive?

If she was part of something illegal, they wouldn't want evidence. She wouldn't be allowed to go to hospital or even to see a doctor. Her readings were so strange they'd have her hooked up to five different machines just to see how she was alive.

Getting tested at the lab must have tripped their sensors.

She looked up from her notepad she didn't remember picking up. It was covered with notes and arrows she didn't remember making.

Everything pointed to Roh. She'd have the security team on the human side run deeper background checks on the rest of the list, but she had that smug sense of having solved the problem already. Due diligence didn't hurt, but she knew she had the right woman.

How would she contact Roh safely? Should she contact her?

She leaned back and stretched and looked over at the clock. How had so many hours passed so quickly?

"Fuck."

This was going to call for strong coffee.

6

OLD MEMORIES

ROH

Roh circled the abandoned-looking building three times and collapsed behind the wall before she could be spotted. There was no way in that she could see which wasn't exceedingly dangerous. The fence around her target building was tall, but that wasn't all...

Razor wire topped the whole parameter.

There was one building nearby that might allow for a jump, but she couldn't find a way in without possibly tripping alarms. That would get her in, but not back out.

There was, of course, no going through the fence. That was the thing of stories. She knew that their security was good enough to detect it. Besides, it was like waving a big flag that you'd been there. The entire point of it was not to be seen and never to be noticed.

This building used to house some kind of medical facility, and probably more. At least it was when Roh was last there, so long ago.

Roh knew her plan wasn't the best. Go back to a place they once used, if they even still used it. It was the only lead she had without begging for help from Benjy. She hoped it was possible she might find a way inside, in hopes of getting lucky and finding her records. In hopes of destroying them before she got caught.

That was three too many hopes. This wasn't going to work.

What she needed to do was pull them to her. One agent in a dark alley somewhere. That might be enough to get some answers.

"Switching plans," Roh whispered to herself from the rooftop that gave her the best vantage point of the factory.

That was when she heard someone at the ladder she'd used minutes earlier. They were trying to be quiet, but in the silence of the pre-dawn, she froze at the sound.

She checked her exits, of which there was only one. What if her visitor had a gun? She stopped that thought before it started and looked for cover instead. Nothing that would amount to more than a few seconds of protection before she'd have to fight.

She looked over the edge, spotting a hedgerow three floors below. Without considering any longer, she jumped.

In free-fall, time has a way of stretching. She knew if she had time to count her breaths and count her heartbeats she had been falling for long enough to break something. The adrenaline hit hard. And she still fell further.

Right before impact, her body went limp as if under a deep sleep. From the ground, it would have looked as if she'd died mid-fall. Instead, she bounced against the hedge, letting it take the brunt of her fall, softening, so the recoil pushed her up into the air. As if part cat, she twisted and landed on her feet.

She felt blood dripping into her eyes, down her neck, and something didn't feel right under her shirt, but none of those things prevented her from running full tilt away from the complex. If they didn't know who the intruder was, her blood would tell them everything they needed to know. But that was something she'd have to worry about later.

————

317A Northfield Court. Not somewhere Roh had wanted to return to, but it was nearby and as safe as anywhere.

Just after 2am. She'd be up, but just barely.

Roh knocked. To herself, she let out a long sigh. She knocked again, slightly louder.

The door opened to someone in a bathrobe. "Roh, you're not taking one step in here. My god, what happened to you?"

Roh just looked at her. There were so many ways to try to start the sentence, but what came out wasn't planned. "Can you give me something so I don't bleed on your doormat?"

The door shut, and opened again. The lady handed her a wet rag, which Roh put to her face, hoping to catch the worst of it.

"What happened, Roh?"

Roh sighed and tried to gingerly wipe where she felt the worst cuts. "They came after me. Broke into my apartment. Took Max's…"

"Roh do not tell me they hurt Dot."

Dot was Rebecca's nickname for Max. She couldn't even remember where the nickname started, but her head was already spinning from a near concussion and no sleep.

"They didn't hurt him, but they did steal his collar. To warn me, I think."

"You look like you tried to take them on."

She shook her head, gently. "Bex, please let me in so your neighbours don't see me. I promise to stay in the entryway. I honestly wasn't sure who to turn to."

The door opened further, and Roh took the hint. As

promised, she stood ramrod straight after she stepped inside. Bex shut the door behind her.

"I did something to piss them off," Roh said as she dabbed at more wounds. "I'm supposed to stay under the radar."

"I know," Rebecca added.

"I guess I broke a rule."

Rebecca's face took on a moment of concern. "So they came and roughed you up to teach you a lesson?"

"No, I'm sad to say, this was my dumbass self trying to think up a plan in the worst possible way." Roh dabbed a bit more at the back of her neck, hoping to get the worst of it before she dripped blood in the entryway.

"You always were a bit hotheaded." Rebecca chuckled.

Roh could only shrug in agreement. "I managed to fall three stories without breaking anything major, but it was close. They knew I was there."

"Where?"

Roh sighed. "Back at the building they used to use as a kind of hospital. I couldn't find a way in, but they still found me."

"And your plan was to go in, find your records, and destroy them?"

Roh just nodded.

"You do realise what year this is, right? I know you were always a bit old-fashioned, but things don't work like that anymore."

Roh felt herself crumble a bit in defeat. "Can I clean up a bit?"

Bex pointed to the bathroom. "No white towels."

"Yes, ma'am."

Roh glanced around the familiar apartment as she carefully stepped towards the bathroom. Just as before, Bex had a variety of stuffed animals, all of them various primates, tucked along the couch and most available surfaces. Roh had always thought it a bit creepy, but over time warmed to them.

She took a minute to thoroughly clean herself, checking in the mirror.

Being clean made Roh feel slightly better. She still desperately needed rest. It was going to have to wait. Besides, being with Bex felt like going backward, even if it was for a short while. Of all the options, she knew she couldn't stay there. She had to leave.

"Roh, stay in the bathroom."

So much for leaving. Like a prey animal, she froze, listening. The right opportunity could come at a moment's notice, but there was little that could be done if they managed to catch her. Stay. Run. The choice sat there in her mind, stretched taut across her body. Each moment she waited might be the moment where her chance disappears.

Not wanting to risk waiting any longer, Roh ignored her ex and rocketed out of the bathroom towards the bedroom window. There was no way she was going to risk a face-to-face encounter, and she knew her way around the outside of Bex's bedroom about as well as she knew her way around the inside.

There wasn't time to think. Instinct took over.

Out to the ledge, then up along a surprisingly strong awning, and then down the emergency access. She'd done it a hundred times before, but never under quite so much duress.

Overhead, she heard the sound of a helicopter she hadn't noticed before. Mentally, she mapped out the city in all directions. Six blocks from her location was a tunnel she could use, if they didn't spot her entering it. That'd be the trick.

What was it Benjy told her? *Eventually, bad blood gets washed down the gutters?*

It was worth a shot.

She took off towards a she expected a manhole to be. She couldn't be sure, but it paid to be a bit lucky.

"Holy shit, yes."

Ten seconds later, she was squeezing herself down onto the ladder, closing the lid overhead.

Darkness.

Her feet splashed into the water at the bottom. She mentally started the countdown. Being in this filth was a great way to ruin your feet.

The torch on her phone showed her immediate surroundings a moment later. From here, she could reach almost anywhere in the city. With a bit of luck, they'd guess wrong and she'd be free.

Her home? No. They'd look there immediately.

Benjy's? Possibly. That'd be a tail-between-the-legs last resort.

Then an idea hit her because it just seemed a bit too ridiculous not to try. There was a gym close to the Bonobo lab. It was part of the chain she was a member of. It should be open 24 hours. They wouldn't look for her there. And, she'd get a chance to grab a shower, work out a bit, take another shower, and eat. With luck, she might be able to get a fresh pair of shoes for far more than she felt like paying. At this point, though, she wasn't about to get picky.

———

Roh's heart was still racing as she dried herself off. As expected, the gym was open, and she managed to kill enough time for morning to rise. Already there was a healthy number of people coming and going.

She thanked the goddesses that she was an easy shoe size, and laced up her entirely too expensive new pair of sneakers.

Sitting on the bench, she felt her pocket vibrate. She unlocked her phone to find two new messages. The first one was from Bex telling her she better be alright.

The second one, much to her surprise, was from "lab cat". Roh furrowed her brow and then smiled at the message. She only knew one person who might message her with that nickname. She made a mental note to ask her name, but she was happy to play a cat and mouse game until then. Little did this nerd know just how not mouse-y she was.

She stood up and pointed to the wall behind the point of sale desk. "Can I get one of those oversized hoodies as well?"

7

TROUBLE IN A HOODIE

JESS

"Dr. Stockwell, there's someone here to see you about retest results?" The formal voice echoed in the office from her open door. There were few things Jess hated more than the messengers they used in the office. It felt ancient and obnoxious. Yet the execs, in their infinite wisdom, had decided that prompt responses were key to business success.

Jess looked up from her tablet, more than a bit perplexed at the disturbance. "The what?"

"The retest results. She says she was one of the lab rats."

Jess put her tablet down and actually made eye contact with the runner. "Please, see her in."

The familiar figure rounded the corner and entered her office a few minutes later. The shape absolutely drowned in an oversized hoodie.

Roh pulled off her hood, her short hair still managing to be a mess of twists. "I got your message."

A chuckle bloomed from Jess. "And you thought to respond in person? Record timing, by the way. I normally have to wait twice as long for someone to respond over text, and here I get you in the flesh."

With that, Jess walked up and shut the door to the office, ensconcing them inside. "Someone is after you, aren't they?"

Roh's face immediately told Jess that this wasn't the direction she wanted the conversation to go. Her response was to clam up.

The scientist turned curtly and took a seat facing her visitor. "Look, I'm not sure if I can help you, but I don't even know what you've gotten yourself into. And I'm *definitely* not sure if I want to be involved once I find out. A date, fine. But this? You look like you got dragged through a thorn bush and slapped on a plaster."

Roh chuckled once, short. "Is that your assessment, doctor?"

"Roh, you don't know me, but I'm going to be honest with you. You look like shit, and it's making me more than a little nervous."

Roh didn't chuckle that time. "I get that. I wish I could say this was a social visit. Trust me, you weren't my first option."

"You're fantastic at making people feel comfortable and wanted, has anyone ever told you that?" Jess said flatly.

"If you'd let me... look I wasn't trying to pull you and your lab into this, but it's obvious you're part of it now. They broke in, didn't they? That's how they knew I'd been here. I'm surprised they even let me in the door, I couldn't even remember your name."

Jess sighed. "We'll add that to the list of security measures that need to be tightened. It's Jess, by the way. Why did you come here?"

The courier pushed up her sleeves, her face a mask. "As bad as it sounds, for a date. For a way to get off their radar for a night. For a place to sleep if things go well. At least... look, I'm not thinking clearly, but there's one thing I know for sure. You looked at my results, didn't you? They're probably why that device didn't work properly. I probably lit up your scanner like a Christmas tree."

Jess could only nod at the assertion.

Roh continued, "Look, I meant what I said. All I was trying to do was get some cover for the night. I wasn't trying to drag you into this. But if you've already seen my records, they're going to want you gone. Yes, that kind of gone."

Jess chuckled, despite herself. "Well now your date idea sounds even more exciting," she said with no small amount of sarcasm.

Roh finally looked her in the eyes, her face tweaked into a smirk. "Are you ever serious?"

"Are you asking if I can be serious? Yes. If you're asking if my life being at risk makes me serious? No. If we ever get to know each other, I'll tell you why. I do, however, want to stay alive. As much as an us versus them romp sounds like it'd be a hell of an adventure, that's not going to be our best way to ensure we both survive. I'm assuming that's your plan. To survive?" She didn't really wait for a response before charging on. "For that, I need information. Who are we dealing with? What did they do to you? What are they planning to do with you?" She paused, but it wasn't to catch her breath. "I know they did something illegal to you, but I can't figure out what or why."

"I can't tell you." Roh's body slumped against the wall.

"Look, we're already in danger if what you say is true. What is telling me going to do?"

"No, I mean, I can't tell you. I don't know." Roh ran her fingers through her hair, and Jess caught herself remembering why she was so attracted to this woman. "They didn't tell me. They only told me the rules. No medicos. They'd contact me when it was time. I've tried to never look back and always look forward. But I fucked up. Something your lab did broke the rule. Now, I have to look back and dodge while I do. I'm sorry. I shouldn't have come here. If I was thinking more clearly, I would have found a safer place to crash and figure things out." She stood up. "No, I'm sorry, Jess. See, I haven't slept in over a day. I have no filter, but that's a separate issue. No, I am really sorry."

"Stop," Jess commanded. Roh stopped at the tone of her voice. "Everything was already set in motion before you got here. If you're right, I was already in danger. They just haven't made their move yet. Perhaps we can slow them down. I have access to a few properties off the book. They won't be able to track records to find them. I'm more worried about you if we're being honest. How did they know you were here? How did you trip the system? Are you carrying some kind of tracking device?"

Roh just shook her head. "I don't know that, either."

"This is something you and I can figure out together. Come with me."

Jess led Roh out the door, up a few floors via elevator, and to a big set of double doors.

"Welcome to my lab."

8

GIRLS THAT GO FAST

ROH

"I could sleep in here." Roh looked around the chamber she found herself in. A fancy grid of foam pyramids, mesh wires, and other things she couldn't identify. The chamber was near silent, enough to make her ears ring.

"Most people don't like the effect. I find it rather soothing. Here, step over here."

"What is that?" Roh looked the refrigerator-sized machine up and down. "Is it going to help you pull the tracker out of my body?"

Jess shook her head. "I'm afraid not. But what it will do is tell us if there's a tracker there to begin with. Stand right there." Jess pointed at an "X" on the floor marked in tape.

"I feel like I'm doing a stage audition."

"Oh right, before we begin, phones off." They both shut off their phones. "And here we go. Let the magic begin."

"What is it?"

"This? This is a top of the line full spectrum analyser. It cost a fortune, but we should be able to ferret out if anything on you is sending a signal back to base."

They both stood still as the machine blinked and the screen

drew pretty colours. They meant absolutely nothing to Roh, but she was content to watch them. There was nothing better to do.

"Can I talk?" she said, finally.

"Yes, it won't affect the test."

"Is this what you do all day? Mess with machines like this?"

Jess checked the readings for a minute before responding. "Yes and no. Machines like this help me do my job, but my job is to think and solve puzzles. These tools help me find the puzzles to solve and, on occasion, help me solve them. But they can't solve the puzzles. That, thankfully, is still in the realm of humans."

Roh chuckled. "I'm guessing you make good money at it, if these are the kinds of toys you get to play with."

Jess opened her mouth and then shut it. She opened it again. "You don't know who I am, do you?"

"Other than a woman who calls herself 'lab cat' in her text messages, and honestly is quite attractive when she lets her hair down."

Jess blushed. The comment caught her so off-guard, it was a direct hit.

"I did mention I'm too tired to have filters this morning, didn't I?" Roh replied. As if in response, the machine emitted a satisfied beep. "What's the conclusion, doc? Am I gonna live?" Roh stared at the screen, again making no sense of the lines and shapes.

"You're clear. I'm honestly a bit in shock. Though, I have a hunch. This next bit shouldn't hurt, but if it does, let me know."

Roh sucked in air. "I love it when I'm the lab rat and they say 'shouldn't hurt'."

Jess handed her two metal cylinders. "Here, hold one in each hand but don't let them touch. Sorry, this is the closest thing I have for testing my theory." Then, as if possessed by some motherly instinct, Jess' hands travelled up to Roh's face. "We're going to figure it out, okay?"

Roh looked down. It was her time to blush. When their eyes met again, her face was beet red. "You're trans?" The words were but a whisper and out of her mouth before she could stop them, and she immediately swore. "Fuck, sorry, I shouldn't have said that. Forget I said that."

On instinct, Jess pulled her shirt back down to cover her belly and the near-invisible patch that sat on it. "I... normally wear multiple layers so that doesn't happen."

"You don't do injections?"

Jess shook her head. "The patches..." Her voice faded as she found Roh's face.

Roh gave her the best nod she had in her. "Yeah, they work better for me, too. Again, sorry. I didn't mean to say anything if you weren't ready to share."

"It's..." Jess began, but then lost her words. "Here, let's start the test."

Roh concentrated extra hard on not opening her mouth for the next few minutes. There was no point in kicking herself. What's done was done. Then, she saw it. Once she noticed it, it was impossible to look away. That same look she'd seen on Jess' face at the donut shop. The look she no doubt tried to hide from everyone, even herself. Those eyes that felt so adrift in the world.

Again, Roh bit back her words, but she couldn't look away. Finally, Jess looked up from her tablet and held her eye contact. They waited, eyes locked on each other, neither of them giving in to the social urge to break the exchange.

Roh lost track of time looking deeply into Jess' eyes. She wanted to acknowledge all those feelings she could see, just by making space for them, not by talking about them.

At last, the machine gave its familiar satisfied beep.

For a moment, Roh wasn't sure if they'd actually let go of the moment, but Jess broke first, turning back to the machine.

"You've got a long-life tracker in you. That means that..."

A fire alarm cut her off, screaming its deafening warning. Lights flashed. The alarm was near deafening in the anechoic chamber.

Jess pushed the machine aside. "Follow me." She motioned to make sure she caught Roh's attention. Roh was only too happy to follow her.

———

Roh gasped at Jess' car. Machines like this lived on fancy billboards or in the store room windows in the expensive part of town. She never imagined she'd ride in one.

She followed Jess into it, hopping into the passenger seat. Jess immediately grabbed something from behind the driver seat.

Roh looked around, her jaw loose as she took in the interior. It was like something out of science fiction, all glowing panels and magic buttons. "You must have made a lot of money on those boner grow devices."

"Yes. Very funny. Here. Recline the seat all the way back and put this on you." Jess handed her a large picnic blanket. Roh did her best to comply with the request, covering her face in the process.

When the car roared to life, Roh felt it in her gut. She never thought of herself as a speed slut, but with this machine around her, she felt things.

Covered and cocooned by the blanket, feeling the rumble and growl of the motor and the pressure of far too many hours awake, she cooked with delirium and arousal. She thought back to Jess in her lab coat. That lonely look she carried just under the surface. Her flirtatious side, and this other side.

Roh had hoped for a fun one-night stand with the nerd, and already she felt a tug. She wasn't sure she was ready for that, but she had to admit to herself that at this point she wanted nothing more than to get somewhere safe, and if vibes allowed, see what kissing this girl would be like. Actually kissing. Kissing with questions and no promises.

As Jess shifted gears, Roh moaned. Her throaty vowels mixed with the deep growl of the engine. She bit her lip. Probably a good thing none of her ex's had something like this.

"You okay in there?" Jess asked. Roh could tell she was keeping her eyes on the road from the sound of her voice.

"Fine, just fine." Roh's voice floated through the blanket. She knew it was her voice only because she spoke those words, but she sounded like a cat in heat.

Jess didn't comment on it and went back to silently driving them to their destination.

About ten minutes later, the car pulled to a stop. "Stay there."

Roh came out of her half-daze as she heard Jess' voice. Rain pattered all around her. For a moment, Roh hoped that Jess would leave her here to sleep in the car under the comfy blanket and the sound of rain.

She started awake at the sound of the passenger door opening. How had she fallen asleep so quickly?

"Let's get you inside," Jess said, grabbing the blanket and holding over both of them to cover them from the rain. Roh matched stride with her until they were well into the apartment building. She silently watched Jess switch and punch a floor into the elevator, riding it up, feeling more than a little vulnerable. Had she made the right choice, trusting the scientist? She'd just been going with instincts, but now she was about to go into this person's home, she wanted to slow things down a little to be sure she had her exits. Thirteen floors up didn't give her many options, and they weren't even at the top floor. Stairs and elevators. She doubted this would be the kind of building with external traversal. Maybe the balconies would be staggered. If she was lucky.

"You okay?" Jess had been watching her. She hadn't unlocked her door yet.

"Sorry, I just... If they come for us here, do we have a way out?"

There, she did it. She admitted what she was thinking and probably sounded paranoid. They would have had to track them all the way here. She had that tracker in her, but they didn't always know where she was, did they?

"Once we're inside, no, they won't be able to track you. Our phones won't work, either. Here, let me show you."

Jess let them inside, locking a series of bolts behind her.

"This is my safe house. Thanks for covering your face, by the way. Now I don't have to swear you to secrecy about its location." Jess chuckled at her own statement. "Signals don't leave this apartment, and I can monitor for anyone coming towards us."

She threw her keys on the table.

"Come in. You can toss the blanket into the laundry room." She pointed to her left. "If you need a shower, there are fresh towels and wash cloths ready. If you need fresh clothes, I think I have some things that might fit you."

Roh just stood in the middle of the apartment and blinked.

It was larger than anywhere else she'd ever lived, or any of her girlfriends had ever lived. And this was just *one* of the places Jess stayed?

"Look, it's no big deal. Come in and make yourself comfortable."

She walked up and grabbed the blanket from Roh.

"Hey, it's really no big deal. What do you need?"

The care in her voice grabbed Roh's attention, and she again found herself looking into Jess' eyes. She made a note to be careful when she did that. There was entirely too much going on in there, and every time made her feel something.

"I'll take a shower," Roh said, forcing herself to break the look. "I could really use a nap after."

"Do you want me to make us some lunch?"

"I would not say no to that, but doesn't your office expect you back? Surely everyone has returned after the fire alarm by now."

"I'll let them know I'm working from home."

Roh nodded and walked into the bathroom, peeling her shirt off as she shut the door with her foot. She admitted to hoping Jess was watching.

———

Roh opened the bathroom door to the light sound of snoring. Passed out, with a tablet on her chest, was Jess. Her hair bunched around the pillow resting on the arm of the sofa. Her legs bent in a way that didn't look comfortable, but it didn't seem to bother her.

There was a tiny bit of Roh that wanted to draw on her face, she had to admit. Old habits die hard. Jess looked really peaceful when she slept.

Making sure to walk gently to the kitchen, Roh looked around for foodstuff and breakfast fixings. She made an oh face looking at pancake mix and maple syrup in the fridge. Time to live it up.

If she ended up waking her up with the sound of bacon

sizzling and pancakes being flipped, she figured Jess wouldn't mind.

As quietly as she could, she set out to prepare breakfast.

"My, aren't we a bit presumptuous? Didn't I already offer to make breakfast? Not that what you're doing doesn't smell good. It smells great."

Jess managed to hold the fake annoyance in her voice, but soon crumbled as she reached over and grabbed a piece of bacon off the plate, happily biting into it.

"I yield. Cook away."

There was something oddly domestic about this kitchen dance. They weren't even technically friends, but it would have been impossible to tell that from how they were interacting with each other.

"Roh?"

Roh looked over her shoulder after flipping the last of the pancakes. "Yeah?"

"Do you remember anything about what they did to you?"

Jess was still munching on the same piece of bacon. She looked like she was savouring it, but her eyes were unfocused, clearly lost somewhere deep in her mind.

"I don't. I was a stupid kid. I agreed to things I shouldn't have to get what I wanted."

"And what did you want?" Jess finished the last of the bacon, chewing slowly. Her voice was still half in a trance.

"I... Look, I lived on the street for years. It took a long time to work up to be as comfortable as I am now, and even that is living week to week. When you know you need to make the change – when you really need to make the change because it's choking the air out of you – sometimes you make bad choices. But, if I'm honest, it's better to be breathing."

Roh slid the plate of bacon and pancakes to the middle of

the table and then set out plates for her and her bacon-stealing breakfast companion.

"Forks and knives are in the drawer to the left of the sink."

Places set, they ravaged the plate of food.

"What... did they give you? For transition?"

Roh swallowed. "Only the basics at first. Meds. They gave me a card so I could get refills as needed. Even just that felt so worth it at the time. Then, they promised when I did what they needed from me at some point in the future, they'd do the rest."

Jess turned to her. "The rest meaning bottom?"

Roh nodded and stood up to poke around in the fridge.

"Have anything you want from there." Jess' voice was welcoming and encouraging.

Roh sat the orange juice on the table. "I'm not even sure if I need it now. I'm so used to where I am. But at the time, it's all I could think about. I think just because I wanted so badly to start." She poured herself a glass, and then offered a glass to Jess. "What's your story?"

Jess chuckled. "I don't know if we know each other well enough for that. It's not a happy one, let's just say that much. We're talking about you, though. You're who they're after."

Roh drained the rest of the orange juice. "You too, now, if I'm right."

"Now, how would you like to burn a few hours?" Jess couldn't hide the smug look on her face.

Roh coughed. "And what happens in a few hours?"

"In a few hours, it'll be lunchtime." Jess laughed at her own joke, though Roh wasn't entirely sure it was a joke. "We need a lab so we can safely run tests on you to find out what they're after. We also need someone who knows what to look for. We can get that, I have resources, but it'll take time. I can make the calls, but then we wait. We're best hunkered down here, moving only when we know where to move to. But, if you have other ideas, I'm all ears."

The tone in her statement wasn't condescending. Instead, it sounded like she honestly wanted to brainstorm.

"I have a friend… we met when I was on the street." Roh started telling the story, then realised it was going to be tricky to thread the tale without sounding like a Mafioso herself. "He's got some connections, but he says I need to work for him. If I do, he'll pull the strings and find out what we need to know."

Jess paused. "That sounds like a *useful* friend to have." Her eyes searched Roh for more, and then she let it go. "That's an option, if you want to use it. I'd feel safer here, but if you want to risk the path you know better, you should. In fact, to make it clear, you're not a prisoner or anything. You should do exactly what you want to do. This was the first place I thought of going, but I'm not an expert in staying out of the way of secret organisations. Full disclosure, I'm also trying to figure out if we can sneak one of my friends up here to have a threesome. It would certainly be one way to spend the time."

Roh laughed. "You're either insatiable or have a curious sense of humour. I honestly can't tell which. Are you seriously ten steps ahead? We haven't even held hands, yet."

"Just something to keep in mind." Jess stood and walked back to the sofa, pulling up something on her tablet. "Let me get things kicked off. If you need anything, let me know."

"What the fuck." Roh whispered to herself while she tossed the dishes into the dishwasher.

9

STEPPING INTO THE UNKNOWN

JESS

Jess knew that using sexual humour to break tension wasn't one of her best qualities. She'd been reprimanded more than once for it. Still, it just rolled off her tongue.

She couldn't help but be hot for Roh. Admittedly, waking up to the smell of bacon in her own home did something to her. A kind of domestic sexual lubrication, and certainly enticing.

She thought she was turned on before, but as she sat up, she saw a generous display of flesh in front of her. Roh was bent over, still in her bathrobe from earlier, picking up something from the coffee table. Jess' mouth slackened as her eyes fixated on what was in front of her. It only lasted a second before Roh stood again.

"Can I ask you a question?"

Jess struggled to anticipate what Roh wanted to know. "Sure."

"Why do you call them Bonobo Devices?"

Jess looked down to see that Roh had picked up one of her spare Bonobos off the table. She flipped it around in her hand.

"Marketing department chose the name. I went with it. Why?"

"It doesn't really have much to do with the Bonobo." Roh set the device back down, this time being a little more careful with her wardrobe.

"How do you mean?"

Roh shrugged. "Can I borrow some clothes while I tell you?"

They walked back to her bedroom at the end of the hall. Jess pulled out a handful of clothes after confirming sizes and stepped out into the hall. They left the door mostly shut between them.

"I had an ex that studied primates. Talked about them all the time. She said that the Bonobos are an interesting study in primate social behaviours. A lot of people just think of them and sex. That's not even half the story." Jess listened intensely, though she was more than a little distracted by the thought of Roh being naked on the other side of the door. "Apparently, the Bonobo evolved complex means of sexual touching to manage social conflict. They use it to avoid violence. In some ways, it's an evolution because arousal may soften that fight instinct, though no one knows exactly how the Bonobo themselves are experiencing it."

The door opened, and Roh stood there. "What?" Roh asked. Jess' eyes were pure fire.

"Roh, can I kiss you?"

Jess could barely hold it in. Seeing Roh in her clothes. Smelling the bacon she had cooked. Hearing her mini lecture on something she clearly cared about.

Roh watched Jess' drag her teeth over her lips. Slowly, Roh stepped towards her.

Jess knew instinctively something in this was a test. A small test, but a test nevertheless. She didn't budge. She felt Roh's hands on her hips. Their eyes locked, and a second later, Roh broke into a smile.

"Yes."

Jess knew that time reached out like tendrils ahead of her. Each choice, a new branch. Each set of choices, a whole new life just ahead. She drew in her breath, waited a beat, and leaned in. Whether or not this was going to turn into something in the future, Jess didn't mind. She was going to take this moment for all it was worth. Tendrils of the future be damned.

Her lips met Roh's, and she put all she felt onto those lips, sending all the signals she could. Though she lacked telepathy, she let her body do the talking.

Roh moaned as if tension just under the surface had found its release.

It was a first kiss. Something told Jess to pull away. To check in. To be sure. Doubly sure. As she did, Roh's eyes focused on her.

"Fuck, you're intense."

Jess startled. "Is that a good thing?"

"Jess?"

"Yes?"

Roh smiled. "Can I kiss you?"

There was no answer, just a mutual rush to taste each other again. As if two beasts, raw, feral, starved of the very thing that gave life its vitality.

Jess felt her back hit the wall, and she gave Roh everything. Her lips, her neck. Wherever she wanted to devour, she granted easy access. Here was someone who matched her intensity toe-to-toe. Oh, how she'd ached for someone who could do that.

She felt herself get lifted off the ground. How fucking strong was this girl? The charge that blossomed between her legs sent electricity up her spine. She wrapped herself around this powerful woman and drank in every affectionate exchange.

Finally, as if coming out of a daze, Jess grabbed Roh's face and joined their tongues. They danced as careful as ballet dancers and then again they ravaged each other, drawn together in the swordplay of tongue and lips that sharpened love's other faculties.

Jess' eyes rolled back in her head as she felt Roh swell between her legs. The very idea of this powerful woman using her girlcock on her nearly made Jess lose her purchase on Roh's hips. Yet, Roh held her strong, rocking her hips so that the friction grew against their most sensitive places.

Roh nipped at Jess' neck, which caused a giggle to erupt from her playful prey. "How is she so impossibly hot?" Jess said, as if asking an imaginary audience.

Roh giggled in response. "You haven't seen anything, yet."

"Holy fuck am I looking forward to finding ou..."

That was all Jess got out of her mouth as she felt Roh grind into her again. Just feeling her raw need nearly rendered Jess speechless.

But she had to say something. She took a breath and wrestled her courage. "Roh? You feel amazing. Fucking incredible. But I can't cum this way."

Roh's face was all hunger and desire as she studied the woman wrapped around her. "How do you want it?"

She stared into this woman's eyes, pausing before she admitted what she needed. "Anal." She said it. So many lovers turned her down, yet she needed it in a way few women did. Almost ashamed of how much. Here was someone who could understand.

Roh leaned in close. Her lips a mere hair's breadth from the ears straining for an answer. Her voice was but a whisper, but it carried the husky hues only queer sex can paint. "Jess, I'm going to fuck your ass until you're so spent, you can't even peel yourself off the sheets. I'll have to carry you to the shower myself."

At that, Jess' body truly gave up any struggle. As if showing her she was fully capable of making good on her promise, Roh carried her to the bed and set her down.

Jess managed a single syllable. "Left"

The left nightstand. As if Roh was now psychically linked to her, she reached in and grabbed the lube and condoms. The nightstand drawer sliding open made Jess salivate, and she tore her clothes off in response.

She was in position by the time Roh came back to her.

Roh didn't rush. She made Jess listen to the sound of her own clothes being peeled off one by one, dropping each on the floor. Jess rocked on all fours, her need growing at the sound of someone having entirely too much fun teasing her.

When at last she felt Roh's strong hands on her back, she let out a long "fuuuuuuuck". Then, at the feeling of Roh entering her, her brain exploded in the rush of being fully taken.

There are so many nerves in that part of the body. So many lovely nerve endings. As Roh filled her, she felt herself stretch to accommodate her girlcock. The pressure at the anus. The hug of the rectum. That tantalising moment right before Roh's pushed against her prostate. Each one caused a new kind of moan, and when her p-spot met Roh's swollen member, she let her know. Oh, she very much let her know. She let the neighbours know, too.

———

Roh held her sweetly in the comedown of their first time together, a gesture Jess more than appreciated. True to her word, Jess' body had gone completely limp by the time they had finished.

"Roh?"

"Yes, Jess?"

Jess turned her head to catch Roh out of the corner of her eye. "I'm not going to give you some line like I've never been fucked like that before."

"Mmmhmmm."

"But it's been exceedingly rare. You're something special. That was something special."

"I'm glad we agree." Roh chuckled, the sound of her voice pleasantly vibrating Jess' back. She found herself wishing she could experience it again and again. Roh adjusted a little. "And after I shower you off, I have a few ideas in how we might - what was it you said? - burn a few hours."

"And I'm the insatiable one?" Jess laughed, her voice flooded with mirth. "I will happily satisfy you in any way you desire. And I mean in any way."

Jess felt Roh's girlcock swell against her ass at her words.

"Oh, she likes it." Jess smiled again.

Roh nipped at her ear. "Yes, she very much does." She leaned back. "Let's get you cleaned up. If you think you can stand."

"I thought a certain someone said she was going to carry me to the shower."

Without a word, Roh hopped off the bed and came around to Jess' side. Seemingly without effort, she lifted Jess into a bridal carry. "You didn't let me forget. I respect that. I like a woman who holds me to my word."

"Do you?" The words had left Jess' mouth before she had thought through exactly what she was asking.

Roh just smiled down at her and walked her to the bathroom.

Jess stood tentatively on the bath mat while her new lover set the shower controls. That glorious sound of the shower head coming on, like a downpour in a forest. Jess noted she was still pretty high from Roh railing her. She stepped under the stream.

"Roh?" Jess turned around to face the naked woman behind her.

Roh looked up.

"Come fucking kiss me."

Always make the shower big enough for two. Ancient wisdom that Jess had taken to heart in each of her apartments. She mouthed a silent 'thank you!' to whoever told her to do that oh so long ago.

Roh's body crashed against hers, the rainfall shower head covering them both with a fresh cascade of warm water, though their bodies were already hot from internal heat.

———

After the shower, they managed to take a proper break, rehydrate, make a snack, and check messages.

"I got a lead on a lab we might be able to use." Jess looked up from her tablet, her other hand feeding herself slices of apple.

"I can't believe you eat apple slices with peanut butter."

Jess chuckled. "You'll be glad at what else I'll happily eat. But listen, the lab is about a fifteen-minute drive from here. It's close. I think we can chance it, though I may pull in a favour."

"What kind of favour."

"I'm going to borrow a car from an acquaintance of mine. He works on all my cars and happily gives me loaners for the amount of business I throw his way. That'll give us something that's decidedly harder to track. He's on his way over now."

"Will it be like your current car?" Roh could barely contain herself in her question.

"You liked that, did you? Yes, actually. Similar, but different colour and last year's model."

Roh smiled. "Can I drive?"

10

AN OLD COMFY COUCH

ROH

Roh was shocked that Jess was about to let her drive.

Jess adjusted her passenger seat and turned to Roh. "Before we go, there are some things you need to know."

Roh gripped the steering wheel and nodded. "Tell me."

"First, that tracking device you have. I want to see what we can do to mute it without giving it away if we can. It would have to work by charging itself off your body, but also likely off any electrical field you enter, say as you walk through a mall and pass through one of the advert portals. Or you drive this car through any toll portal. Which reminds me, no toll portals."

Roh chuckled. "Obviously."

"Okay, that was the big one. As long as we avoid anything that will trigger your tracker, we should be able to get there without them spotting us. Unless they've hacked into traffic cameras."

"If so, we're pretty much out of options," Roh completed the thought.

"Right, let's go."

Roh cranked over the engine, enjoying it as the feeling of power ran up her legs.

"Don't kill us," Jess joked.

"Safe as houses."

Roh put the car into gear and pulled out from the parking spot.

Jess sighed. "I'm glad you're driving. I've only slept 15 minutes in the last day, and I'm starting to feel it."

Roh laughed. "That's more than me. What was the second thing?"

Jess turned and stared at her without speaking. Eventually, she relaxed back into the seat.

"I asked them to bring us something to sleep on. Told them we'd likely pull an all-nighter."

"You want to crash out when we get there?"

Jess braced herself. "Roh, please don't say crash while you're the one driving."

She didn't reply, instead she reached over and fondled the gear shifter. Jess kept looking over as she did it, and Roh couldn't help but grin at her. It would have been cute, but she looked like a cat about to cause trouble.

———

"Holy shit, where did you learn to drive like that?" Jess stumbled out of the car, her body a mixture of adrenaline and exhaustion.

"They teach every runner how to drive. Best way to get out of a tight spot in a hurry. But I've never driven anything like that beast before," Roh gestured to the car as she tossed Jess the keys. She fell in behind Jess as they made their way into a new building.

They entered a large lab even more full of devices than the last one. Jess walked up to a similar fridge-sized machine. "I'm going to set this to run while we're resting." She looked over at Roh, who was curiously investigating a tray of various tools.

"Don't worry, I don't think I'll need to use any of those on you," Jess joked, though her voice carried a hint of seriousness. "Are you not tired?"

Roh looked up and shrugged.

"Huh. Well, that makes one of us. But I've got work to do. Get some rest if you can, and I'll wake you when I have something useful. At least here in the lab, they shouldn't be able to track us. The whole lab is shielded. We couldn't let anyone snoop on our research, now, could we?"

Roh found a well-loved sofa in the corner of the lab, no doubt worn threadbare by too many long nights in the lab. Or *other things*, knowing Jess.

She laid down and closed her eyes and tried to slow her spinning thoughts.

It had to have been hours that Roh stared at the back of her eyelids without getting anything remotely like sleep. Every once in a while, she'd steal a glance over at Jess, who was working feverishly at something.

When Roh finally managed to fall asleep, her respite was brief. Standing over her, beaming and looking rather proud of herself, was the scientist.

"You look like you managed to figure something out," Roh said flatly.

"I think so, but it's going to take some time to train it. Here, sit up a minute?" Jess motioned and let Roh pull herself into a sitting position. "I know this looks a bit cumbersome, but it's all I could do on short notice."

Roh looked down at what Jess was holding. It looked similar to the Bonobo Devices, but thicker, with a huge chain that looped through it. "What is that?"

"This, I hope, will be enough to block the signal so they

can't find you wherever we go. It'll be a bit heavy, but seeing how strong you are, hopefully that won't be a problem. The trick now is that it needs to go through a training phase. If you put it on, I'll attach it to that machine over there. With luck it'll take less than six hours, but it may take longer depending on when your tracker tries to call home."

Jess watched as Roh took the device and pulled the chain around her neck. It felt a bit silly, so Roh instinctively pulled her collar up a bit to hide it as much as she could.

"One sec." Jess stood and ran a cable between the large fridge-shaped machine and her new necklace. "Okay, now we wait. And I, for one, am ready for a snuggle. You up for it?"

Roh nodded, a bit perplexed.

Instead of scooching in, Roh carefully levered herself over Jess, squeezing in between the back of the sofa and Jess' body.

"Mmm, that's nice. I bet you don't often get to be the little spoon." She laughed as she wrapped an arm around Roh. "Doesn't every strong, sexy snack like yourself secretly want to be the little spoon?"

Roh chuckled and laid her own arm over Jess'. "Funny enough? No, we don't."

Jess purred into her lover's neck. "Roh? Did I ever mention how good you smell?" Jess had buried her face into the crook of Roh's neck.

Roh just smiled and held her. In a few short minutes, her breath came in nice, even waves.

Roh shut her eyes, and waited.

Her thoughts were a mess of worries. People in the underground she always remembered to dodge. People who had screwed her over.

Next, like a long list, other thoughts filled her head. Contacting a neighbour to look after Max. And then what she knew about this scientist.

She wasn't sure how much she should trust Jess. Not because Jess was giving her any reason not to trust her. She just wasn't from her world, the same world these assholes were operating in. She was a straight-laced, albeit not *straight*, lab tech inventor nerd who made good money in a way that made the tax man very happy. None of that was Roh's world. What was going to happen when push came to shove? Would she be streetwise enough to actually help, let alone stay alive? Roh wasn't sure. Watching her back would be just one more way she'd end up making a mistake.

Yet here she was, wrapped in her arms, in a lab she asked for specifically to help Roh out. It was obvious that she didn't know the streets, but she knew this world. To Roh it was nothing but flashy screens and mysteries, but it meant something to Jess. She sounded so confident she could help. Maybe she could.

Roh considered slipping out while Jess was asleep. She always considered her exits. Should this be just a one-morning stand? Roh could take her chances with Benjy. It's possible he was pulling her along to try to get more work out of her. It's possible. Though that wasn't really Benjy's style. He must know something.

The real question was would Benjy turn on her if the offer got good enough. That thought made Roh pause. He absolutely fucking would. Money is money. Streets are streets. Bad blood might wash into the sewers, but so did good blood if you weren't on the inside.

Roh let herself feel Jess in her arms. It was a bet. She knew it was. They might come up with nothing. Something Jess did might tip off this shadow group and leave them backed into a wall. A million other things could go wrong. Part of Roh wanted to fight for this. Wanted to see where things could go.

Even a street kid knew when someone felt like more than a good fuck.

Roh relaxed into the silence punctuated by Jess' breathing. If her instincts and her heart seemed to be pointing in the same direction, she better listen. She knew it wasn't going to be easy.

Then again, nothing ever was.

At last, Roh's own tiredness finally caught up with her, after listening to Jess sleep for the better part of an hour. Like a fine line of light just ahead of her that only her mind could see, she felt herself pulled into a dreamless sleep. Her ears stayed active, her skin still sensing every sensation, every breath of her lover in her arms. Her eyes, closed but ever at the ready. She slept the same way she'd slept since they changed her. That operation. Those lights. The sound of each machine as they worked on her. They never fully left her mind. Not until she slipped into that paper-thin state of oblivion.

11

THINKING WITH THE BODY

JESS

Jess opened her eyes slowly and froze. The girl who had managed to whip her into a hell of a crush was only inches from her face. This woman's arm held hers firmly. It was a heavenly way to wake up.

Jess wasn't sure she could call it a crush. She wasn't sure what to call it.

Whatever the label, she sure as hell could feel it.

Just the sensation of this woman against her sent little shock waves under her skin. Jess had felt this before when she was younger. Though there was nothing like this in recent memory.

She tried not to overthink it, but thinking was her bread and butter. The trouble was knowing how much thinking was enough.

Jess quietly chided herself. She'd already started over-thinking.

What did her meditation teacher tell her? *"Think with your whole body."* She was pretty sure at the time that the teacher said stuff like that to fuck with her. You could only think with your brain and perhaps have some kind of ancillary thinking apparatus of the nerve clusters around your body. But thinking with your *whole body*. Nonsense.

Still, she was never one to pass up a challenge. She tried it. What did it mean?

As she meditated back then, she remembered settling on the idea that the whole body could be partitioned into separate systems, and each one could vote. For example, if asked "how do you feel?", she would need to stop and collect data from all the parts of the body that had a vote. How does the heart feel? How do the lungs feel? And so on. She couldn't answer the question completely without doing it. Sure, you can give an answer, but without checking in, you're not giving a whole answer.

Right now, her heart felt something. She just wasn't sure she wanted to give it a vote. Her crotch wanted to throw in its vote, too. As much as she did love to indulge its direction, she wasn't sure she wanted that vote, either. She looked up and caught the curve of Roh's lips and thought back to their first kiss. It was only a handful of hours ago, and yet, it felt like weeks had passed.

Everywhere tingled. She knew she should wake her up and check the results and see if the experiment was a success. She also knew just how tempting it would be to wake her up gently. Softly. Those lips.

Those fucking lips. They wanted to be kissed.

She realised anthropomorphising this sleeping woman's lips was maybe a bit of projection.

She was the one who wanted to kiss them. Wanting felt like such an insufficient word. Craved. Like food or sex. Craved the sensation of touching their lips once again.

The scanner emitted its happy little beep.

The sound was almost enough to pull Jess out of her reverie. That was, until Roh opened her eyes and set her gaze on Jess'. This wasn't the first time their eyes had locked, but something happened each time they did. Jess felt it in her belly. That growing urge to do anything - absolutely anything - for this woman she barely knew.

"...did you sleep?"

The woman was asking her a question, and Jess fought back control of her mind. "What was that?"

Roh smiled at her. "I said, 'how did you sleep?'"

"Well, I think. Shall we see what your results are?"

Roh didn't break her gaze. Instead, she let her voice drop into that dangerously sultry range that voices play in when there is something very particular on the brain. "If we must."

Jess wanted very much to cancel everything and make out with this woman until they died of thirst. Or until they passed out. Whichever came first. Instead, she felt herself be lifted from her position against the back of the couch to a squatting position in front of the couch in one graceful motion. The act made her more than a little wet.

"I'll... I'll go check on the machine." Jess stood on unsure legs and forced herself to walk to where she could see the screen.

Jess read the numbers off the screen. "I think we've got something."

Roh got up off the couch, careful to hold the cable attached to her necklace, and walked up to her.

"Here, we don't need this anymore." Jess reached up and unhooked the line from the modified Bonobo. "Though to be sure, we should stay here for another few hours. I want to make sure your tracking device is truly silenced. Also, we need to eat. Are you hungry?"

"Definitely. Thirsty, too. How long have we been here?"

Jess wasn't sure. When she was working, she rarely thought about eating or drinking until she felt dizzy. "I'll get them to bring us something, but we'll need to stay in this room until we know for sure we're in the clear."

Jess punched a few things into her tablet and set it aside.

"While we wait, I want to show you something." She pulled up something on the screen attached to the refrigerator machine and pointed.

"To explain what's going on, there are two things we need to talk about. Antennae and their power requirements. And the human body as a battery."

Roh chuckled humourlessly. "Going with the classics, I see."

"And this doesn't make sense for the same reason that movie didn't make sense. But I'm getting ahead of myself."

Jess motioned at a graph with an upward bending line. "Antennae are power-hungry things. To reach large distances, you need much more power. This is why big radio stations also have to use a lot of power to broadcast. You have an antenna in your body. They need to power it so that it's strong enough to send a signal, and in return, we need to time our own blocking mechanism to stop it. Your antenna is surprisingly strong."

"Because of the power thing?" Roh ventured.

"Exactly that. Human bodies do generate some amount of energy. The body then uses that to power itself. It's not trying to waste that power. Now, your body is generating a significant amount of additional power to feed into the tracker for its reporting out."

"Hence the needing to work hard to block it?"

Jess nodded. "That's it. No doubt, we'll raise suspicions once you stop calling home. But it's the best we can do, I'm afraid. At least they won't know where you are."

They heard a knock. Jess grabbed the bag and shut the door behind them. They ate, sharing bits of trivia about themselves when Jess wasn't hopping up to check something on the computer.

At last, she turned to Roh. "That might work." She gently pulled at her collar and checked the device. "Does it fit okay? Not uncomfortable?"

"Well, I slept with it on, so that probably means it's not too bad." Roh smirked.

"Right. Right, of course. Just wanted to make sure it wasn't too snug."

At that, Roh gave her a mischievous look. "I seem to recall you quite enjoyed a snug fit." Jess felt the comment stir her insides. Then, Roh's hands cupped her face. "That's a good girl. You know, your face is so expressive."

Jess melted. She was sure someone had cranked the temperature in the lab a good fifteen degrees.

"You win." She didn't have the will to pull away from this woman and not let her get an advantage. The second Roh took initiative, Jess was hers.

The kiss, though, sent Jess' mind into overdrive. She imagined what kind of tests they had done to her. High metabolism, optimised calorie expenditure, high base bioelectrical output, less need for sleep. These were just the things Jess knew about. She looked at them like a puzzle, trying to understand how they fit together. Were they trying to turn Roh into some kind of super soldier? A fighting machine. She hadn't seen any indication, yet, that Roh was a fighter. Well, except for being exceptionally strong and flexible. Jess added those to the list she was forming in her head.

The feeling of lips left Jess', the feeling of her bottom lip being sucked lingered.

Her attention snapped back into the present moment. "I thought that might get your attention. I asked what our next step would be."

"I have an idea, if you're feeling brave enough to try it."

"What do you mean?"

"Let's see if anyone chases us if we grab takeaways on the way back to my place." Jess gave her best confident smile.

Roh tilted her head. "Is this what you call science?"

Jess smiled. "Something like that."

"I have my own theory I want to test." Roh's voice was frank and earnest.

"What's that?"

Without a word, Roh kissed her again. This time a moan immediately escaped Jess' body, and she pulled at Roh's until it was flush against her own. She hungrily wrapped her arms around her and held her tightly.

Just as before, Roh pulled back slowly, sucking on Jess' bottom lip as she did. "Just as I thought."

Jess looked at her quizzically.

"You're a much better kisser when you're paying attention."

They chuckled together. "That's fair. It's easy to get distracted sometimes."

"I noticed. Shall we?"

As they walked out together, Jess felt Roh pull her close. "So," Roh began. "Am I your new product, now?"

"You are certainly my intense area of focus."

Jess noticed how absolutely perfect it felt to have their bodies pushed against each other.

"Food," she said, her voice feeling just as distant as her heart, as it was swept along in the wave of emotion just under the surface.

Roh nodded. "Yeah, food."

For one moment, it felt like a test to see who would let go first. Eventually, they both did, relaxing where their hands and held their bodies together.

It was Roh who spoke first. "Let's go see if this device actually works."

———

Jess felt like she was holding her breath the entire drive. Not from Roh's driving, she had shown herself to be more than adequate driver, while also obviously enjoying it thoroughly. Not from the device, either, though she admitted being a little nervous at first.

What was worrying Jess were the unknowns she didn't know. She never truly got used to them. She could play it confidently, be the tough girl when she was surrounded by expectations. That mask was always a constant companion. If she let herself take it off, though, she knew her own limitations all too well.

The smell of chicken caught her attention. They'd managed to get to the restaurant without issue and were now heading to one of her places. The scent of the food helped relax her, or, at the very least, make her salivate a bit more. It was a welcome distraction.

That was, until Roh's voice chimed in with a rather unnerving sense of worry to it.

"Jess, I don't think this thing is working."

"How do you know?"

Roh checked the rearview mirror and took a sharp left turn at the last possible moment. She checked the mirror again. "We're definitely being followed."

12

THE VARIETIES OF POWER

ROH

"Fuck." Roh let out a hiss as flashing lights filled the car. An unmarked police car by the look of it. As fun as it would be to see if she could outdrive the police behind them, something told her that this wasn't the time to run. Her instincts often steered her right, so she'd long ago learned to trust them.

Jess wasn't entirely sure.

"How do we know the cops aren't working with the group out to get you?"

Roh was a little impressed she was suspicious. Too often, when she met folks that were comfortable in their lives, they were all too willing to roll over and show the police their belly. They knew *they* weren't the ones in real danger.

Jess pulled out her phone, opened an app quickly, and set it on the dash. "Hands on steering wheel. Don't say anything. I've got this."

Roh complied with the first part, but was definitely unsure about the rest of what Jess had said. Had she really had that much experience talking to police? Should she fight her on this one? She chanced a glance over at her passenger. Jess' face was a mask of perfect confidence. She had done this before. She'd had to steel herself against authority before. Roh made a mental note to ask her about it, that is, if they made it out of the next ten minutes without going to jail.

As the officers approached the car, Jess reached up and tapped the button on her phone's screen.

Jess rolled down the window and put her hands back on the wheel. Before she could greet the officer, the phone beside her came to life.

<Greetings officer, I am Automated Legal Entity 9843E7-9. You will be corresponding with me for the duration of the vehicle-based enforcement inquiry.>

Roh heard the officer swear under this breath.

<This conversation will be recorded and logged at both The National Legal Document Preservation Centre and with the Administrative Registrar for this district.>

At that, the officer went silent for a moment.

"Ma'am, please produce your licence." The officer used a nice, even tone. Roh could tell it was directed at her.

Before she had a chance to move, the ALE jumped into action.

<The humans using the Automated Legal Entity have requested the extended form of vehicle-based enforcement inquiry. Under the extended form, you will need to first produce probable cause for vehicle operation inquiry. Under this procedure, please state why the car is under police investigation.>

"We pulled you over because you're currently driving a vehicle registered to Danway Drexel of Danway's Advanced Auto Services. You are wanted for questioning in relation to his disappearance."

<Are either of the humans in this car under arrest for the disappearance of Danway Drexel of Danway's Advanced Auto Services?>

"I can confirm they are not under arrest at this time. Both

are requested to be taken to the precinct for questioning. Now, can I please do my job?"

Roh tensed at the officer losing his cool, but she tried not to show it.

The stop went about as expected after that point. After checking documents, both Jess and Roh were required to follow the officer to the precinct. They'd allowed them to stay in their car, as the car was registered with the police escort services.

Roh realised they wouldn't have been able to run if they had tried. A few button presses, and the cop would have just driven them straight to the precinct himself.

As she let the car drive behind the police car automatically, she let herself exhale a long sigh. The night was still far from over. The sound of someone happily munching away at dinner drew her attention.

Sure enough, Jess had opened the bag and was working her way through a juicy-looking chicken sandwich.

"Want a bite?"

Roh took one, even though she didn't really feel hungry. Just the act of sharing food like this, regardless of the situation they found each other in, felt endearing. A moment later, her stomach reminded her that yes, indeed, she was exceedingly hungry. She fished her own sandwich out of the bag.

"I figure we might as well finish this off before we get to the precinct," Jess said before carefully licking the juice running down her hand. "Grab some chips, too."

Roh marvelled at how calm Jess was. She looked like she didn't have a care in the world.

Jess chomped on a few hot chips. "Wish we'd ordered a shake, too."

"Still hungry?" Roh said, managing to finish her sandwich one bite later.

"Ever try dunking chips in a milkshake?"

Roh laughed. "No. No, I've definitely never done that."

"You should try it. It's quite good." She continued munching away at the chips.

"What do you think happened to Danway?" Roh asked, reaching for a chip. She could tell Jess was slipping into thinking mode. She doubted she'd do much food sharing if she ate in that mode.

No response.

A minute passed and Jess looked up from her automatic chip consumption, the bag nearly empty. "If Danway is smart, he got out of town. I can only hope. Look up, we're almost there." Her voice changed from serious to sarcastic. "Now, look, there's something important to remember that my trans big sister told me years ago. Don't be the horniest person in a room full of strangers."

Roh laughed. How in the world was she this relaxed?

"We'll be okay," Jess said, turning to face her companion. "My lawyer will already be there waiting for us, thanks to the ALE"

"You might have mentioned that when the car was automatically locked and taken control of by the police officers about eight minutes ago."

Jess shrugged. "True. That's fair." She chuckled to herself. "I meant it as a surprise, but now that I say that out loud, it sounds a bit ridiculous."

The car pulled to a stop. The police officers escorted them to the precinct.

Roh gasped. It was like walking into a Bonobo Device convention. At least ten separate couples were arguing with police, all proudly wearing their colourful consent devices.

"That's a lot of bad dates" Roh said, watching the crowd. Then, she looked over at Jess. Her lover was ignoring the gathering and had her eyes searching elsewhere.

"She should be here."

A moment later, Roh replied. "I think she is."

Through the front doors stormed a firebrand with hair to match. Her suit was taut and tailored, expensive, and fuck-you in all the best ways. Roh had no doubt that if Jess had a lawyer, this is what she'd look like. More than a little, Roh also wondered if this was the third in the threesome Jess teased her about.

"Hi Jess, sorry I'm late. I got your message when I was halfway into a lovely... Hi Roh, Jess has told me so much about you. Hello, officers Johnson and Kennedy, let's go ahead and get started."

Roh's head spun. It was like the woman didn't require oxygen when she spoke. Roh watched as the officers ushered them forward, seemingly already familiar with this tornado of a woman.

Once they were seated in the interrogation area, the solicitor fired away. Her name, it turned out, was Regan. She said her last name and credentials too, but they all ran into one syllable and Roh couldn't make them out. She explained they had only a passing acquaintance with the missing and that there was no further inquiry necessary as both were logged as in the building by the building security system, whose records could be made immediately available if necessary. Roh only tried to open her mouth once, but made no sound and shut it without protest.

After ten minutes, fifteen tops, the redhead named Regan had ensured their release and promised to track down any additional info on request.

Roh's head still felt rather spun as they exited the building.

"Look, I'm famished," Regan said, pulling open her attorney briefcase to fetch her keys. "I was mid-snack, and it left me peckish, if you know what I mean. Would you two be interested in a bit of a dine-in?"

"Does she mean...?" Roh ventured, unable to finish the thought.

"Oh, she is quite clever, you're right." The lawyer spun on her rather expensive heels, appraising them both. "Interested?"

"Maybe... later?" Roh chanced, looking over at Jess, who nodded her approval.

"Perfect. You know where to find me." With that, she was off in what felt like a poof of smoke to Roh.

"She's quite something," Roh said as Jess slid their arms in together.

"She's also quite effective." Jess didn't say much after that, instead walking with Roh back to the car. "I'll drive this time, you look a bit dizzy."

Roh tossed her the keys, and they climbed in.

"You sure you're not at least a little peckish?" Jess asked, turning to Roh. She let out an uproarious laugh as Roh's face turned from frowning to crimson.

13

CLEANUP IS IMPORTANT

JESS

Jess put the car into drive and pulled out of the police parking lot. She stretched her hand over and rested it on Roh's thigh.

Roh went from looking a bit distracted to making the sound Jess would have called a purr.

"Do you want to stay at my place tonight? If you don't want to, I understand. It's just been a bit of a day. I figured we might want to get an early start of it tomorrow with the next round of tests."

Jess felt Roh thread her fingers into her own as they rested on her thigh. The sensation was so warm, it nearly arrested Jess' attention away from the road.

"I want to go back to yours."

To Jess, it sounded a bit tired but also something else. Something of wanting to be there together. Something of possibly more. She was afraid to admit to herself how much she wanted it, and how much she was noticing her own projection whenever she watched Roh do something or say something. She wanted more from this woman, but it was way too early to ask.

Instead, she relaxed and kept her hand on Roh's thigh. "You got it."

She drove the rest of the way in silence. When they returned to the safe house, which Jess was secretly hoping was still safe after the kerfuffle with the police drawing attention to where they were, she let Roh in and watched her cross to the bedroom and pull out clothes for sleeping.

Jess listened.

The faucet came on. The sound of brushing. All the little domestic sounds were melodic notes to her ear. She longed to hear what the whole chorus sounded like when it all came together.

If Roh was heading for bed, Jess wasn't going to let her sleep alone. She slipped on a pair of pyjama pants and crawled on top of the sheets, grabbing the tablet off the nightstand. Without a word, Roh came up to the bed in bare feet and pyjamas and crawled in against Jess, resting her arm across her, her head on her shoulder.

Without even a good night, she was out. Her light snore felt like a cool balm to Jess, who let the tablet illuminate just enough to get some reading in.

Moving as little as possible, she pulled up her search box and typed in "Bonobos" and then relaxed, balancing the tablet on her leg.

———

The next morning started off innocently enough. Jess awoke to find that the tablet had been closed and set on the nightstand, along with her glasses. She'd been tucked in at some point during the night with a blanket.

From the kitchen wafted an assortment of tempting aromas. Jess smiled. She very much could get used to this.

"Feeling better?" she asked, as she came into the kitchen and wrapped her arms gently around the front of the focused chef.

"I do! Sorry I had to crash out last night. I guess you were right about the day being full. Also, can I just say, you're cosy as fuck."

"Likewise." Jess leaned her head against Roh's amply strong back. Goddamn, this woman could get her stirred up so easily.

"Breakfast will be ready in about five minutes." Roh's attention was on something in the skillet.

"Five minutes, you say?"

Without another word, Jess dropped her right hand until it found the bulge, softly covered by the borrowed pyjama bottoms. She tightened, smiling as she heard Roh hiss at her touch.

"I'm doing my best to thank you," Jess teased, her head forehead pushing into Roh's back. She felt Roh get hard in her hand, which only drew her attention more to her work.

"Fuck." Roh's voice was but a hoarse whisper, her bottom lip bitten as she sucked in air. "I think you're testing me to see if I'll burn myself when you distract me."

Jess' hand froze its movement. "Do you want me to stop?"

"No." Roh's need rose to the surface, motivating Jess to start moving again.

That's how they stayed, Jess stroking her lover through her pyjamas. Moments passed and the hardness grew. Roh grabbed the counter with both hands, which Jess took as her cue. She squeezed and pulled, then reached and bit the back of Roh's neck and she pressed her further and further.

Hearing Roh's release was better than any coffee in the morning. She couldn't care less what mess she made or where it landed. She'd do it again. And again. Until this goddess of a woman begged her to stop.

Roh spun on her and lifted Jess off the ground, eliciting a squeak. She carried her to the kitchen island and set her down, then attacked her lips with her own.

Jess wrapped her arms around her lover's neck and chuckled as their lips parted. "Was that a thank you?"

"It was. It also was a *don't start something you can't finish* warning."

"Mmmm, fair. So what are we having?"

"First? Food. Before it gets cold. And then you are going to clean me up."

Jess swallowed and looked Roh in the eyes. That fire and mischief was such an intoxicating combination. This woman was fully capable of breaking her in half, and the thought made her more than a little wet.

"Come on, hop to. We've got things to see and people to do." Roh lifted Jess off the island and set her on the floor. "Grab us some plates?"

The lesbian lust puddle that once was Jess oozed over to the cabinet. She reached for the plates one at a time, setting each carefully on the countertop before willing her arms to fetch the silverware. She wasn't sure how she made it to the table with the necessary dining accoutrements, but it sure didn't feel like it was by walking.

After breakfast, without ceremony, Roh pushed away from the table. "Come on, you've got a mess to clean up." She walked into the bedroom and stood in the middle, facing the hall.

Jess felt her whole focus collapse down to only this woman. She was realising she would do anything Roh asked her to do. The thought didn't scare her. Not even a little bit.

She walked towards Roh, letting herself lock eyes as she approached. Once in front of her, she dropped to her knees. From there, she reached up and peeled down the pyjama bottoms. They'd stuck a little to Roh's leg; she pulled them down and gently as she could. Next, she reached up and worked her fingers under Roh's underwear elastic. Again, they'd stuck, and she did her best to gently separate cloth from skin. The mere act of pulling down the cum-stained panties turned Jess' cheeks crimson. She marvelled at her lover's girlcock.

Jess set to work on it, licking it from every angle, then pulling the whole thing into her mouth to suck hungrily at it. Each moan. Each vibration. Each twitch. All of them felt like they were wired directly into Jess' brain.

Jess couldn't help but push her luck just a tiny bit. While she lavished the girlcock in her mouth, she reached around and grabbed Roh's ass. Roh in turn rewarded her with more of the moans she craved. She had to push it further. With one hand freed, she trailed along the lovely curve of the ass cheek until she felt her finger slide between them. Just a tease is all she wanted to give. Just one, good, delicious tease.

As she pressed her finger against Roh's puckered flower, she felt her lover fight to keep her legs strong. Exactly the reaction Jess wanted. She even moaned against Roh's growing member in thanks.

Just to try to fuck with her as much as possible, Jess timed the push of her lips and throat with the gentle push of her finger at Roh's entrance. At that, Roh finally had to grip Jess' shoulders to keep standing.

The bliss of service poured into Jess' mind, and she let herself go completely blank with it. She was here, in this moment, for one goal. She wanted to see what Roh was like fully unknit and drained.

When Roh finally came, Jess desperately tried to memorise the sound. It was like warm honey, a throaty chorus of feminine pleasure. Jess happily drank each and every bit she could draw from her weakened companion.

Seconds later, Roh crumpled to her knees, her legs spread and squeezing Jess' legs with her own. She crushed her lips against Jess, tongue and thirst and hunger all wrapped into each kiss.

To Jess, it felt utterly sublime.

———

Jess shook her head as they walked into the lab later that morning. Too many fresh images of being in front of Roh on her knees, feeling herself get lifted and taken to the shower once again, and oh the shower.

This girl was going to ruin her. In the best way possible.

"Jess, turn around." Roh's warning shook her out of her reverie. Jess looked up and saw the entryway had more than a dozen men in suits. They looked anything but hospitable.

She froze. Roh yanked her backward, and they launched into a run.

They burst back through the door, nearly tripping in the effort, hurdling themselves towards the car.

"Jess, throw me the keys."

Jess didn't argue and did what Roh demanded, then jumped into the car. Roh had the car in gear in a second, and tore out of the parking lot. Jess spun around and caught the men pouring out into the parking lot after them.

"Holy shit!" Jess' assessment wasn't exactly astute, but it sure captured the feeling of her heart beating its way out of her chest.

Roh was a machine. Jess marvelled at her as her face melted into a steel mask of concentration. She wore it so well, too. As if she'd been trained for this.

For not the first time, Jess wondered if she was fucking someone who was trained for combat. Maybe she was a sleeper agent of some sort. Or some kind of super soldier. She did manage to keep remarkably fit and could pick her up with ease.

The jerk of the car pulled Jess' attention back to the present as she instinctively latched onto anything she could to keep upright.

"We need help." Roh stated these three words in the same calm, level-headed demeanour her face held. "I need to take us somewhere we have a decent chance of being safe."

"Where's that?" Jess asked, her head swivelling from the driver to the two cars trailing them close behind.

"Underground."

The beast of an engine growled under Roh's skilled hand. She soon lost track of where Roh was taking them. All the while they were trailed. Jess knew it was only a matter of time before they got caught.

Jess watched Roh take a dark side alley which turned and dipped down, dumping them out into what looked like an underground parking area. She had never known this was underneath the city. That was nothing compared to what Roh was about to show her.

Roh kept driving. Once they turned into a side tunnel, she shut the lights of the car off, driving in near pitch black as the tunnel seemed to have lost power.

The cars behind them had lagged just enough trying to figure out which tunnel was the right one that they seemed to have missed which one Roh had picked.

Jess spun forward and immediately bit her lip hard enough to make it bleed.

Roh was driving. In the dark. And making sharp turns at all the right spots. Jess wanted to ask if she just knew the way or if she actually could see in the dark, but she couldn't manage to pry her own jaw apart. To call the fear coursing through her body terror felt like a horrific understatement.

"You know, the Bonobo use sexual touching as a way to calm each other when upset."

Jess gaped and tried to respond with *what the fuck?* but only managed the last word, the entire idea of inhaling enough oxygen to speak a full phrase seemingly impossible.

"Fuck?" The single syllable left Jess' mouth with a heavy dose of confusion.

"Not exactly fucking, it's more like sensual or sexual rubbing."

Jess spun on her, her eyes searching for anything in the darkness that would grant her access to know where Roh was. It was only the memory of where the voice came from that told her anything.

Every doubt in Jess' mind wanted to burst forth. Here was someone she wasn't sure wasn't a psychopathic super soldier driving in pitch black like she had some kind of magic power to see in the dark. And on top of it, she was weirdly calm amongst all of this, reciting facts like they were at a dinner party.

How had Roh not gotten them killed ten times over?

"How?" was all Jess managed. These one-syllable questions were at the very limit of her mental capacity. Every brain cell, every neuron, was absolutely choked with fear.

"Hold on a second, it might get a little bumpy."

At that, Jess passed out.

14

GOING UNDERGROUND

ROH

Jess went silent. Dead silent. In a panic, Roh reached over and felt for Jess' pulse to make sure she hadn't killed her. It was a definite possibility.

After confirming Jess was still alive, Roh let out a sigh. She wasn't sure how she was going to explain all this when she came to, but that would have to wait.

"Stay with me, babe." The words were out of Roh's mouth. In the silence of the car, she heard herself use a word with a woman she had known for less than a week. She couldn't afford to think about it. She had to drive.

It wasn't far now, another five minutes or so, and she'd be at the Sun Hearth's underground entrance.

It was possible one of the people following knew the way. She wasn't the only runner. They could have easily hired another runner. They'd have to know where she'd go, though.

She reached over and held Jess' hand as she drove, taking comfort in its warmth, and she took them into the unknown.

The garage area of the Sun Hearth was lit enough you could find parking, but not so brightly that anyone who'd took the runner tunnels would be blinded by it. She pulled into a spot, then came around to Jess' side, opening the door and then carefully unbuckling the seatbelt. Gingerly, she rocked the unconscious woman until she could pull her free from the car. She shut the door with her knee and walked Jess to the elevator.

The elevator opened onto a very red-faced associate, who spun to see who had just come up.

"No dead bodies, Roh. You know the rules."

Roh shook her head. "She's not dead. She's just passed out."

"No one who isn't a runner, either."

"I know. I know. I'm here to work. She's going to help me."

Roh knew this was going to be a stretch to sell, both to the organisation and to Jess, but she had run out of options.

"Is Benjar here?"

"No, he's out. You know he doesn't come to the Hearth unless it's a special occasion." The red-faced person seemed hassled by even having to explain any of these details. "If you're going to work, you better wake her ass up and sign in."

Roh tipped her unconscious companion to the floor, holding her up so she could stand. "Jess? Jess, it's time to wake up." She lightly slapped her cheek.

Jess fluttered her eyelids.

"Easy. We're in a new place. Somewhere you've never been, but I'm going to show you around, okay?"

Jess looked at her, and Roh felt her heart skip a beat. Now it was her turn. Jess was in her world.

"Roh?"

Roh smiled back at her. "Yeah, it's me." She had to fight the last syllable she wanted to add after *me*. Hard.

"We made it?"

Roh gave her a very light chuckle. "Yes, we survived. We're alive. Come on, we've got to get signed in." Roh led her into the alcove's office.

"Roh? What's happening, where are we?"

Roh finished closing the door to the office. "I took you to the first place that came to mind that I had a chance of protecting us." Roh bent over and signed her name on the sheet. "I told them you were with me."

"Where are we?"

Roh thought about a dozen ways to answer the perfectly reasonable question, in varying degrees of truth. She looked up at Jess, trying to gauge how much she could say, not really having the heart to lie to her.

"We're at my previous employer's office. One of them, at least. This is the central one. From here, we should be able to move a bit more freely. That is, if we work."

Jess tilted her head slightly. "What do you mean work?"

"I mean work for the organisation. We have to do jobs. As long as we're steadily doing jobs, we can stay here under their protection. I'm sorry, Jess, this is the first place I thought to come once we knew we'd been made at your lab. They might know about this place, or they might not, but it at least gives us a chance."

Jess looked down at the paperwork Roh had just written on. "I'm going to take it, this isn't a legit job, even though that looks like legit paperwork."

"Everything on the streets is varying degrees of legit, even the cops." Roh leaned her weight on one of the straight back chairs. She watched to see how Jess took her honest appraisal of legality.

Jess looked a bit more at the paperwork, then pushed it aside and looked back at Roh. "What does it mean to work? To do jobs?"

"We get assessed. I've already been assessed, but they'll need to assess you. Once you're assessed, you're given tasks that you should be able to handle and be successful with. I'm a runner, and good runners can get pushed pretty hard, but they aren't trying to kill us. They're trying to do business."

Roh hoped she was at least more convincing than she sounded to herself. She'd done jobs before where she had doubts they expected her to return. But it was business, always business. Cold, but once she expected the cold, it didn't bother her so much.

"And they want me to do jobs as well?" Jess' face was an impossible mask of tweaked eyes and lips. Roh couldn't tell if she was interested, curious, or repulsed.

"We'll both need to. If we do, they'll put us up here. It's not a permanent solution, but hopefully it gives us time to plan rather than just run."

"Roh?"

Jess' voice suddenly held an unexpected level of vulnerability, as if she'd been caught out without food and shelter and Roh was the only one who could give it to her.

"What is it?" Again, Roh fought not to add a pet name to the end of the question to help console this woman she knew she had growing affections for.

"Are we in this together?"

Roh looked up at Jess, having realised she'd let her gaze drop to the floor during their conversation. What was she going to say in return? How much could she share of what she'd been feeling? What her heart felt like when she heard Jess go silent in the car. What her hand felt like to hold.

Roh felt the feelings stir, and she could feel Jess come up close to her. She felt Jess drag a thumb across the corner of her eye. Tears.

"Roh?"

Roh knew she had to say something, but everything she wanted to say felt laced with fear and doubt. How could she say how she felt when things were so early? Their situation so unstable? Maybe they'd both end up in jail, or worse.

"Roh?"

It was a whisper now. Jess studied her face.

Roh couldn't take it anymore. Whatever happened, wherever they ended up, she had to take the chance. She had to show there was more going on here than fucking the hot scientist. There was promise, but there was more. Roh didn't know if it would work, but she was going to put all she felt in what she was about to do.

She moved her head and closed the gap between them, sealing their lips together with the salt of a tear and all the feelings she could send. She pulled at her head, anchoring Jess against her. Not wanting to let her go. Not wanting her to feel any doubt in this moment where she stood. Who she stood with.

She had no idea all this emotion was just below the surface, how her feelings had built so much in the last few days, but now she was going to show the scientist what she had. To give her all the data.

Jess met her kiss and gave as fiercely as she got, pulling at Roh's side as she knocked the chair out of the way.

They heard a throat clear at the door and managed to peel apart from each other. The red-faced associate had returned with a handful of paperwork. "This is for your friend. Roh, be sure to sign it, too."

Roh grabbed the bundle and the associate left.

As Roh handed the paperwork to Jess, she let her face relax just a bit. "Yes. Yes, we're in this together."

———

Roh spun at the noise as she heard the door open. Standing there, looking rather proud of himself, was Benjar.

"Roh, I wasn't sure I'd ever see the day. I had to come see it for myself. So this is the woman who got you back? More valuable than your dog, I take it?"

Roh was quickly regretting her decision to take Jess here. What was done was done.

"Benjy, this is Jess. Jess, Benjar Octillion. He…"

"Will be overseeing your task assignments for the foreseeable future," Benjar finished, his voice dripping with self-satisfaction.

Fuck.

Goddammit.

Roh knew she had totally and completely fucked up. Benjy had been just watching and waiting until she needed him and oh did the spider have that kind of patience. Water under the bridge. Blood down the drains. Bullshit. He was absolutely, thoroughly enjoying himself. That made Roh more than a little nervous.

"Benjar was it? I haven't gotten to meet many of Roh's friends." Mouth agape, she stared back at Jess. How could she not tell this man was the embodiment of all that was snide and slimy in the world?

"Oh, we go way back. Now, let's have a seat so we can read over your paperwork. I'm sure it's right as rain, but we'll need to know where to get you assessed."

Roh stared as her nightmare unfolded in real time in front of her face. Benjar pulled up a chair and sat across from Jess, who was all too willing to hand over her paperwork.

"This looks good. Yes, I think we have a place for you. Oh. Roh? We'll need your signature, too. Right here."

He was loving every fucking moment of this. To Roh's

horror, he folded the form to the last page and slid it in front of her. He pointed at the line that said 'Established Guarantor'.

The thought of signing Jess' life away now came fully into view. They could leave now, make a run for it. Try their hand with the cops. With Jess' lawyer. Maybe Jess had other powerful friends. Roh's thoughts rambled, but there wasn't any use. Jess didn't live in this world. She didn't know how to protect herself. Her resources came in handy, but it was time for Roh to step up.

She put the best, most confident look on her face, grabbed the pen, and signed.

15

ICE CREAM WITH A TWIST

JESS

Jess thought the assessments were surprisingly fun. Not something she at all expected. How fast could she navigate an unlocked computer. How quickly could she correctly guess a password based on clues in the room. How quickly she could understand an unknown technical device. Compared to biohacking and correctly reading subtle shifts in biometrics, this stuff was pretty easy.

That was until they threw her into hacking school. It was like seeing computers from a direction she'd never thought of. Infiltration, she quickly learned, was its own art. The puzzles got more and more complicated, running her brain into overdrive. Luckily, Roh was equally busy with her deliveries. It felt like Benjy was aiming to get his due for protecting them.

After a week of security training, Jess' mind buzzed with all she'd learned. Each day, she expected Benjy to put her into a job

When the call finally came, it was simple and to the point. "I need you to go to the financial district, find a network that responds to this name," he showed her the name on the back of a card. "Then, I want you to do your magic. I'm only looking for one thing. Leave everything else alone."

Just like that, she was about to fully jump into Roh's world. So, she did the first thing that came to mind: she messaged her lawyer.

> *"I might need your help."*

Regan, like always, immediately flicked back a response. "Do I want to know what you're into?"

> *"The cop stuff might have been just scratching the surface. I can't tell you much now, but I might be off the radar for a hot minute."*

"You know where to find me."

That was it. No moral chiding. Just at the ready, like always. Jess suspected that's exactly where she was about to need her.

She looked back over at her notes for her first assignment. They'd split Roh off for the day, so she was on her own for this one. That gave her an idea.

She pulled up the secure messaging system again.

> *"Reg, do you feel like getting your hands dirty?"*

"Always." The response was immediate. Jess knew all too well the answer was also all-inclusive. Jess smiled.

> *"Do you have a disguise, by chance?"*

"I have many. In the mood for anything in particular?"

> *"Something that doesn't look like you. Oh and you'll need to borrow another car. One that can't be traced back to you."*

"The more you talk, the more fun this sounds."

Jess thanked her lucky stars that Regan was anything but a straight-laced lawyer. Her laces were certainly not straight. Nor was the rest of her. But she knew how and when to bend the rules in a way that nothing and no one broke. That's what Jess always found the most impressive. She knew how to thoroughly work a system and come out on top, all with the minimal amount of ancillary damage.

> *"We're going to go for a ride. Oh, do you like ice cream?"*

————

Jess pulled out her phone and checked herself in the selfie camera. They'd done a good job inside. The wig looked spot-on, and the makeup made her face look noticeably different. All told, the look would likely let her pass through a crowd without being noticed and only her closest friends would recognise her. If that.

True to form, Regan was waiting for her.

"Let me get this straight. Err, gay. We're going to drive around the financial district, like we're a pair of tourists. We're going for ice cream. All while doing some laptop shenanigans I probably legally should know nothing about."

Jess nodded. "That's a pretty good summary."

"Are we up for takeaways after?"

Jess knew the question was going to come sooner or later. She considered it. Would Roh mind if she took Regan out for some fun? They said they were in it together. Did they say exclusive?

She mentally shook her head. That didn't feel right. If nothing else, consent and transparency meant something.

"I..." Jess started, but then realised she wasn't sure how she wanted to end that sentence.

"Oh, you two are an item? Don't fuss one whit. I'd be happy to make a house call if you want to share. No pressure."

That was it. True to form, Regan started and ended her pass with equal grace.

"Do I want to know what we're looking for?" Regan asked as she took another turn to complete part of a loop.

"You do not. I know just enough to be dangerous, and if I'm honest, that's already too much."

Regan nodded almost imperceptibly.

"Next street go straight, and then turn left at the next light." As Regan followed her instructions, Jess punched a string of commands into her laptop. "This is where the fun begins."

Jess' computer emitted a quick beep. Then two in succession.

"Do you want me to cover the laptop in a blanket or something?" Jess asked, her voice serious. "I wouldn't want you to be asked in court what I'm doing."

Regan chuckled. "I doubt I would be able to tell them if they asked. Law? That I can do. Computers? Biohacking? Network engineering? Nope, none of the above, I'm afraid. I definitely didn't notice you wiresharking across a variety of networks."

"Goddammit." Jess snorted. "You really should have kept your nose a little more clean. Might help you stay out of trouble."

"Where's the fun in that?" Regan said, shrugging. "Besides, if I had kept my nose clean, I don't think I would have found my way into the prohibited part of the library."

"Or the underground tunnels at the university. Or into the exam test questions. Or, I hasten to add, in between the thighs of quite so many coeds." Jess kept typing, no longer trying to hide what she was doing or what she was looking for.

"A woman has her appetites." Regan focused on her driving. "Which way next?"

"Okay, I think we're close to where it should be. Once I get a lock, we'll park and find something to eat while we wait."

Regan chuckled. She gestured at the seemingly impossible amount of ice cream vendors mixed among the financial towers.

"I would have thought that coffee would be more popular than ice cream?"

Jess giggled. "That's because you haven't checked the flavours they sell around here."

"And I'm dying to find out."

Three beeps, in rapid fire, shot from Jess' laptop. "Here, park around here. We'll let this run for a bit."

They found a parking spot, paid at the parking meter, and made their way towards one of the shops. Regan reached up and roughed Jess' hair as they went.

"This is fun, Bucky. It's almost like old times, except I've got a nicer car."

Jess looked up at her and smiled. "And you don't do the undercut anymore."

"You know, I'm still rethinking that decision. Oh, how I loved my undercut."

"It was certainly better than that time you tried to grow dreads."

Regan held the door open for Jess, then followed her in. "Don't remind me. At least I had the good sense to shave my head after that. Got a lot of dates with a shaved head, I might add."

Jess' mind flashed back to rubbing Regan's shorn head while it was strategically placed for maximum pleasure, then tried to shake the image out of her head.

"Take your pick." Jess gestured at the ice cream cabinet. A moment later, her face broke into a big smile as Regan's cackle echoed in the parlour. The proprietor appeared less than amused.

"I'm sorry, are we in a chemist shop?" Regan hastily scanned the flavours on offer. "Caffeine? Nicotine? Sildenafil?! Isn't that for..."

"Yup."

"Oh my god!" She exclaimed, and then smiled. "Okay, I was trying to pretend innocence, but this isn't my first Financial District ice cream."

"You're such an ass." Jess couldn't help but chuckle. She turned, again amazed at how preposterous the ice cream scene in the Financial District had become, but the stream of hopped up clients seem to say that it was good business.

Jess gasped as her friend pointed at both caffeine and sildenafil. "One scoop of each, please. Bucky, what do you want?"

It hit Jess that Regan was using her nickname for her as cover, too. Clever.

"I think I'll be boring and have the tea cocktail. I still have work after this." She turned to face Regan. "And if there's anyone who doesn't need your particular cocktail of an order, it's you."

Regan just smiled back like the cat that ate the canary.

"Oh, I'll need it." She nodded with her head at a table behind Jess. Jess tried to be sly about turning around to look, but she felt just as awkward as she did when they were both freshmen together.

"They're cute," Jess admitted. The bright eyes and sun-drunk glow definitely was quite the draw.

"I figure in case you get distracted, it's good to be ready."

They paid for the ice cream and sat down at a table, making sure that Regan had a good line of sight for the two women she'd picked out.

"You ever want to do more with the Bonobos," Regan asked as she shovelled ice cream into her mouth with a little spoon. "I mean, imagine. You've got consent figured out but what about enhancing the experience? Giving people a taste of being a little less inhibited?"

Jess blinked at her friend. "Reg, I'm going to be honest. That sounds like a terrible idea."

"Hear me out, right? If they stimulated whatever gland needs stimulating to loosen us up a bit – not violent and awful or anything. I mean, like, peace love and flowers and enjoying a good time while still being able to stop and smell the roses. Picture it. You move next door to new neighbours. Gone are the days they give you the cold shoulder! You're instantly a part of their lives because they actually see you as someone they could have fun with."

"Yes, I'm sure granny will be pleased when her new neighbours want her over for dinner." At this point, Jess wasn't sure if it was Regan or the ice cream concoction doing the talk.

"No, that's not what I mean, at least not quite. We see each other as like a person here, a person there, right? We're all just like marbles in a big game, occasionally bouncing into each other, but no one really knows what the game is. People make all kinds of mistakes because they don't really see each other. I mean, actually see each other. Sure, yes, I mean sex. And appreciating the many forms of sex and non-sex. Hear me out - what if we could loosen the inhibition that holds us back from seeing other people as..."

"Marbles?" Jess cut her off, but she couldn't help herself. "I honestly don't know where this is going. You know some of that is to keep us distanced from people who would prey on us, right? We don't need to get to know everyone intimately if it takes up too much brain space and makes us vulnerable to people who would manipulate us."

"But!" Regan held up her mini spoon with a solicitor's finality. "What if people didn't want to take advantage of others? You know how they feed the sharks in the aquariums so that the sharks don't eat anything else while the kids watch them swim around?"

"You want me to stimulate 'glands' to keep shark people fed so they don't mess with non-shark people, and they somehow also leave old ladies alone. And also everyone is magically more friendly with fewer hangups."

"Precisely!"

Jess shook her head and scraped at her ice cream bowl. "You sound like Roh. *Oh, you should make something that actually is closer to what the Bonobo do in the wild. Bonobo devices don't really work like they do.*"

Regan studied her for a minute. "So what you're saying is that it's a good idea."

"What I'm saying is you should stick to law, luv." Jess pushed her empty ice cream bowl aside and shook her head. She looked up and noticed Regan looking over her shoulder. "Are you going to get their numbers?"

Regan just smiled. "I already did."

If there was one thing Regan was good at, it was all the latest tech. She wasn't above buying products from Jess' competitors if it gave her any advantage in the dating scene.

"You're going to have to tell me about this telepathy trick later. For now, we should get back to the car."

16

ONE GOOD JUMP

ROH

Roh was going to kill him. After this job. She couldn't believe she'd let Benjar talk her into this. She was going to kill him. That was, if he didn't end up getting her killed first.

She stared out at the building she'd tried to enter not even two weeks ago. Here she was, armed with all the info she needed to get in and get out. In theory.

"You wanted answers, kid. That's where you'd find them."

She wanted to fight him. It was too risky. How did Benjar know they had enough info to do this? She looked down at the sheet of instructions. How to get into the building she couldn't get into last time. What time to go, what window to go through, what rooms to search. It would be a long jump - longer than Roh was comfortable making on anything but her best days. Just as she had guessed, the jump lined up through a hallway, catapulted over the railing, tucked over the top of the barbed wire fence, and folded into a roll.

It was a ridiculous move.

Roh had to admit, it also sounded ridiculously fun. That is, if she pulled it off.

The whole thing was a terrible idea. A terribly alluring idea.

If Benjy was right, hidden in the same complex she had scouted out were documents on what they'd done to her. It felt a little too easy, but then again, sometimes things just are.

Roh chuckled to herself. So easy. Just have to make a jump with a slim margin for error, not get spotted, scale a building with an unknown difficulty, get in a window without being noticed. And that's just the outside part.

She looked back down at the paper and committed all the steps to memory. No mistakes. A single misstep, even a single bit of bad luck, was easily jail time or far worse.

Roh readied herself, measured her steps to the window, and checked her angle. Any loss of momentum would likely do her in and send her tumbling to the razor wire head-first.

It was stupid, she knew that. But without risk, there was no reward.

Her heart beat slowed just enough as her mind grew blank. As if propelled by the sound of a gun announcing a race, she shot forward.

Shoes slapped against linoleum and then carpet in perfect rhythm. Her body pitched forward just so as she approached the window. Three jumps chained into one. One from the floor, one a push from the windowsill to the railing, and the last she let herself fall forward just slightly before pushing hard with both feet in musical synchronicity.

She sailed over the fence, her body taking on the gentle curve of a gymnast as she arced towards the safe ground on the other side.

Today, she noted with some pride, was one of her best days. The roll wasn't quite as silent as she would have liked, but she rolled and stood uninjured, which was as much as she had dared hope for. Instinctively, she checked her modified Bonobo to make sure she hadn't knocked it off.

Without missing a beat, she looked around and gauged how best to scale the wall in front of her. The ledges and trim in the wall turned into a blueprint in her mind, and she charted a course through it.

The climb was dry and uneventful, thankfully. With the least bit of rain, it would have been far more dangerous. In short order, Roh was to the designated window. It was locked, but only momentarily, As she pocketed her handy tool, she reached back to the window and slid it open. This one shouldn't have alarms. Benjar promised they'd looked into it. Having people on the inside of security installation companies was certainly helpful.

Holding to the window, Roh listened for a distant alarm sounded or thundering footsteps. Neither came.

She pulled herself through and shut the window behind her. Two steps later, she knew something was horribly wrong. Three people were standing at the end of the hall and one of them turned to look her way. She had to make a decision quickly: jump away from the door or stand perfectly still. The problem with the latter is the human brain dedicates an awful lot of itself to recognising human shaped things. Standing still wasn't an option.

With her left foot, she stepped out of the line of sight with her back to the door. She looked around, swearing all the while. There was no good cover here. No closet, no ceiling escape. Nothing. If they took steps towards the door, she couldn't go back out the window without getting caught.

She ran the numbers in her head. There were at least three of them. Even at average build, that would be the upper limit of what she might be able to handle. More than likely one would get a lucky hit in.

Roh felt her adrenaline kick into gear as the teeth of the trap came into view. To scale down the wall quickly was out of her skill, and she couldn't afford a drop from this height without anything to cushion the fall below.

She willed her heart to slow and focused on being as cold and uninteresting as possible. Even the smell of her sweat might be enough to subconsciously attract their attention. She wanted to be nothing. Of no consequence.

She heard footsteps approach the door, and she pushed herself further into her trance. She figured if they did catch her, given the limits of the room she was in, they would be able to capture her without issue. Her only hope was to disappear.

Heart rate dropped lower and she stood, barely breathing, as the employee walked near the entrance.

"These things don't just stop working. You need to get eyes out there. Yes, if that means talking to the doctor, you do it. We don't lose things in this office. That's not how it works," the voice explained to the others nearby.

Roh didn't even let herself blink. Without moving, she scanned the room again. An old style filing cabinet, a bookshelf, an old office chair, heaps of boxes for paperwork. A stapler.

To Roh's surprise, the voices turned and went down what sounded like a perpendicular hall.

Roh stayed perfectly still until the voices had died to a distance whisper. Only then did she let herself breathe a small sigh of relief. There are three ways to get yourself killed, she remembered: letting yourself get hit, letting yourself fall, and giving yourself away. Some of that training still stuck with her.

Three doors down, take the right hallway, two doors in your left and take the second door. Roh pictured the turn and what the doors would look like in her head. She pictured what her likely exits would have to be if anyone caught her along the way. She wondered if any of the doors were locked in case she needed to duck in quickly, all the while hoping the room beyond was free of surprises.

Her room, she knew, should be empty. "Should" be the ever-present, ever-dangerous operative word. The getaway vehicle "should" be there. The spotter "should" have eyes on the operation at all times. The girl you like "should" like you back. Roh paused. That wasn't on the list. At least not any list she'd really put together. Yet, here she was, thoughts of Jess finding their way into the corners of Roh's mind.

No time to tarry, Roh chanced a step and a peek out the door. She listened. No one was nearby. Confidently, she stepped out, repeating her directions to herself.

She made it to the four-way hall and turned right without issue. If anything, the halls felt eerily empty. She found the door to the room she needed to unlock. Another chill hit her. The only thing that pushed her forward was her desire to find what she was looking for.

Roh stood in the room and shook her head. Two minutes. Tops. Something was definitely wrong. This place should not be as quiet as it was, almost as if the place had been evacuated. Or maybe there was a meeting on a different floor. It was possible.

Roh wasted no time jumping to the backup paperwork. If her source was right, her paper backup file would be here in the cabinet. As quickly as she dared, she threw open the drawers and searched. Three draws later, she found the R's.

No time to read it. She had thirty seconds, at most. Instead, she pulled up her shirt and stuffed the folder into the band that ringed her pants.

She turned and froze.

"Find what you were looking for?" a voice said, sending chills straight down her spine.

17

I HAVE A BAD IDEA

JESS

"Fuck!" Jess screamed as she looked down at her computer. Benjar had messaged her, but it wasn't instructions for what to do after getting the select people in the financial district. It was a short, and heart attack-inducing, message.

"Roh in trouble. Go to warehouse. 4th and Cobblestone."

"I'm on it! We're pretty close" Regan yelled as she looked up from reading over Jess' shoulder. She threw the car into gear. "I used to date a girl in that neighbourhood. But this is not the time for that story." With that, she went silent, focusing on cutting each turn tightly as she wove their way towards the warehouse.

Jess didn't feel the car as it tore through the city towards their destination. All she could feel was her blood pumping in her ears. "Fucking Benjy. Roh knew he was going to try to screw her over."

Regan's tone was crisp with seasoned professionalism. "At least he gave us an address. At least we can go find her and help her."

"If it's not too late." Jess hadn't meant for that sentence to leave her mouth.

Regan didn't say a word. Instead, she just reached over and put a hand on Jess' leg. Something she'd done dozens, maybe even hundreds, of times over their many year friendship. Just that assurance let Jess relax, if only a little.

Jess let out a long sigh of air. "Let's do this."

Regan returned her hand to the wheel and focused.

Minutes later they were in front of what looked like an abandoned multi-story warehouse. The chained gates barred entry.

"Fuck," Jess spat. "How do we get in?"

Regan was looking up at the fence. "How the hell did she climb that?"

"I... don't know. But that's certainly not something we're going to do," Jess said as she craned her neck to get a better look.

"Want me to ram it?" Regan's question struck Jess as perhaps a little eager to be a daredevil, but in the moment she relished the energy.

Jess forced herself to focus on the plan. "Look, there's two of us and who knows how many of them. If we barge in there, we won't be the ones with guns blazing. She's going to have to come to us. A sign, anything. The second we know where she'll be, ram away. Benjy can fucking eat the costs, all the costs, for all I care." Jess turned her head to the left, then the right. "We should see if there's another way in. At the very least, hopefully we can look through some of the windows. We might get lucky."

Regan put it into gear and started a slow circle around the outer parameter. Try as they might, they could barely see in any of the lower windows. If Roh was in there, it seemed a fair chance she was in one of the upper floors.

Jess' face turned into a devil's mask as she turned to Regan. "I have a very bad idea."

Regan smiled. "You know me. I like very bad ideas."

Jess fished in her pocket and pulled out a multitool and then set to work on the front panel of the dashboard. Seconds later, she had it pried free.

"You're reminding me of the old days," Regan joked. "We haven't had a joyride in a while."

"Probably because last time we did, you thought it'd be a great idea to bring two drunk coeds with us."

Regan's smile grew. "That car probably reeked for days."

"Stop talking or you'll make me gag," Jess retorted, though her voice betrayed a hint of sarcasm. "Time to do some really stupid shit."

Regan watched as Jess moved wires from one place to another. She moved with such speed, soon Regan was shaking her head. "I never did know how you knew what to do. Isn't every car different?"

"It is." Jess was deep into focus and only managed to answer Regan's question out of reflex, but then she fell silent. Roh needed her help. This wasn't time to be chummy with her old pal. This was time to do something drastic. A few moments later, Jess straightened back into her seat. "Cover your ears and push the horn with your elbow."

"I don't want to know what's about to happen, do I?"

"You do not. Cover them tight."

18

WHEN COLD FEELS WARM

ROH

Roh opened her mouth and was immediately deafened by an immense racket loud enough to shake the building. On instinct, she yanked her arms free from the agent who had grabbed her.

Another horn blared its way through the halls. Roh wasted no time, shooting past two more would-be captors on her way back the way she came.

A nearby door swung open as she passed. Roh caught a glimpse of people holding their ears, but she didn't slow down.

What she was about to try wasn't going to work, she knew, but she didn't have a choice. Freerunning was all about knowing exactly what your body can do. Exactly what physics would allow. She already knew what was possible before trying it, yet there were only seconds to make the call and she had no other option.

She charged through the room she'd originally entered and headed towards the window at full speed.

"Fuck!!"

The only thing below that was about to catch her was definitely not something she wanted to catch her. Still, it was better than the alternative.

In the split second she had, she tried to picture the jump in her head as she tightened the coil of her body. Minimise damage. There was nothing else that could be done.

As she launched herself through the window, she heard heavy steps behind her, the sound of yelling muffled by the adrenaline pumping through her ears. No freerunner would ever attempt what she was about to. No one ever should.

She kicked off the ledge of the window, sending her into a gentle tumble in the air, tucking herself as she fell.

There was no way from her angle to ensure she would clear the razor wire. None.

As Roh fell, thoughts raced through her mind. Despite her efforts to concentrate on her fall, her thoughts drifted back to being taught how to tumble, how to fall, how to time her runs, how her body moved in the air, how it bounced off walls, how her muscles felt as she latched onto rails, what a city looks like when all of it becomes a playground for the well-trained artists of movement. She thought of Jess, too. Her face devilishly looking up at her when the thought entered her mind. She hoped she'd get to see it again.

The razor wire cut like death into her flesh. Her arms erupted and immediately felt wrong as she left chunks of herself behind on the deadly blades.

Blood. Her final thoughts were of how much blood she was going to paint on the ground below.

———

Roh deliriously thought it poetic that the first word she heard when she came to was "blood". It was difficult to tell, but it looked like a woman hovering over her. Something about this woman felt familiar, but then she decided she hadn't actually awoken yet.

Dream woman seemed to be gesturing and yelling. *Don't worry, dream woman*, Roh thought. *Don't worry, I'll be fine. I just have to lie here and rest for a while. Maybe bleed out a bit more.*

It wasn't that Roh wanted to die. She'd spent too long surviving and clawing her way through each day to give in like that. But when the sirens call the boats to the rocks, at least one of their calls might be the right one. Roh smiled to herself. She imagined the sirens were really pretty. She couldn't remember if sirens had tails, but she wasn't picky. She was sure they'd at least be good kissers.

Something rocked her body in a nauseating way. She wished she could throw up. *Fuck the sirens*, she thought as her mind emptied of the beautiful vision, only to be replaced by whatever this all-consuming disorientation was.

Roh was sure she was dying.

She'd been in scrapes before, but this felt different. This was the wrong kind of warmth and cold. Like a book she read one time where a camper had hiked up a mountain, only for the snow to fall unexpectedly. The author said that the first thing you feel as hypothermia kicked in was how cold you felt. Then, you felt how warm and cosy. And that, he said, was the dangerous one.

Roh felt dangerously calm. Like that siren, she felt something calling to her. *Just sit down in the snow. It's so warm here. Just sit down and relax a while.*

With her last bit of willpower, she tried to force her eyes open one last time to see what all the fuss was about. Surely, it wasn't as interesting as these beautiful maidens calling her to the rocks. Surely. But one look couldn't hurt.

Roh forced an eye open and caught a glimpse of something

more alluring than any maiden she'd ever seen. The look of love and concern on this woman's face nearly stopped her already-fading heart. She looked so familiar.

Roh thought of how nice it would be to have someone look at her like that when she wasn't quite so sleepy. A bit of a shame to see someone beaming at you, wearing their heart on their sleeve, and not be able to reach up and give them a hug.

Speaking of hugs, Roh noticed her arms were on fire. Internally, she shrugged, she doubted she would need them for much longer.

Goodbye, kind lady, Roh thought. *I think it's time for me to go back to sleep.*

A WORLD WITHOUT SENSE

JESS

"She's dying! Somebody help us!" Jess yelled at the emergency entrance of the hospital. As she caught sight of triage running towards them, she chanced one more look down at Roh. The girl she had touched in the most intimate of ways now was almost unrecognisable. Her face a sea of scratches, her arms torn down to the muscle, her clothing not much but tatters.

She almost dared not to touch her, worried that even the act of touching her would push her over an edge she'd never return from. She'd never seen a human body take abuse like this before. Roh looked like she'd been hit by a car. Jess shivered. Not many bodies survive being hit by a car.

The workers were there. They mentioned something about grabbing legs to help her get on a stretcher. Jess followed their instructions automatically, her body already slipping into shock as the weight of what she'd witnessed hit her.

She knew Roh was special. She'd never known anyone who could take a fall like that and have a chance to survive. Jess even remembered marvelling at how gracious she looked in the air, before all hell broke loose.

Regan was around her. Then Jess was standing. There was a waiting room, but she didn't remember getting there. A hug. Something warm to drink that had no flavour. The sound of wheels passing. Voices.

Jess blinked and shook her head, hoping to clear it enough to give meaning to everything that was happening. It wasn't any use.

Regan hugged her tighter. The pressure felt nice. It was really the only thing she could feel at the moment. Normally, her brain disconnected from her body so it could work harder. In that moment, Jess couldn't even feel her brain. Thoughts felt lost in an ocean of worry that had pulled her completely apart. She wasn't sure what she would do if Regan hadn't been there to be her anchor.

Jess was vaguely aware of the cops as they stood around, talking to Regan. The whole time, she didn't let go.

Her brain fought to reboot, but Jess felt broken. She folded herself against Regan, tucking her head between Regan's chin and collarbone. Someone wrapped a blanket around them.

When the overwhelm in Jess' brain finally slowed, she had no idea how much time had passed. Regan was still there holding her. They were still wrapped in a blanket. Someone had brought her coffee, but it didn't look warm.

"Reg?" Her voice sounded hollow and distant, as if spoken through an array of cotton balls.

"Buttercup, you're awake."

Jess pulled back from Regan. "Oh my god, fuck off with that."

"You are definitely awake." Regan chuckled. "She's still in surgery. They said they have her stable, but she'll still be in there for longer."

"And the cops?" Jess could feel her head clearing.

"They're going to want to speak with her when she wakes up. I can be there with her when they do."

Jess sat up and held the blanket against her.

"She also had this on her. It's torn to hell, but maybe it's useful in some way?" Regan reached underneath herself and handed Jess a torn folder generously spotted with blood. She felt herself slip a little back into her trauma brain as she looked at the blood.

Regan pulled it back. "Sorry. I wasn't thinking. It can wait." Regan lifted up and sat back on the folder.

Jess leaned over and put her head on Regan's shoulder. "How much longer do you think they'll be?" she asked, her head still feeling both heavy and dizzy.

"I don't know, but I'm sure they'll tell us the moment they know. The cops are going to want to talk to you, too, now that you're no longer in shock. I'll be with you the whole time."

"About the last thing I want to do is talk to the cops."

Regan nodded gently, her chin lightly resting against Jess. "You and me both, hun. Luckily, I get paid to do it."

"What do you think they'll charge her with?" Jess wasn't sure she actually wanted to know.

"It's hard to say. It depends on what these people press charges for and how much they want to show their hand. Trespassing, at the very least. Breaking and entering and destruction of property are also possibilities." Regan ran her hand up and down Jess' back in slow strokes.

"Do you think she'll go to jail?" The question felt fragile in Jess' mouth.

"I don't, actually. And not just because I'm a damn good lawyer. Something feels fishy in ways that have my senses tingling. For one, where are the g-men? We saw them as Roh escaped, and then they disappeared. No one chased us. No one showed up at the hospital. My guess is that by the time the cops get around to checking out that building, it'll be empty."

Jess sighed. "Why does that sound so scary in my head."

"The unknown is always scary, babe. If it wasn't, it'd be the known."

Jess wasn't entirely sure Regan's sage wisdom made any sense, but she let it go. The vibe felt sufficient.

———

Jess had just finished her second cup of coffee when the nurse approached them. Jess looked up at her expectantly.

The nurse's uniform was starched and immaculate. "Roh is resting in intensive care, and she's awake. You can see her, but please limit your visitation time to twenty minutes or less."

They followed the nurse into the intensive care unit and then to Roh's room. She looked even worse, if that was possible. Her skin was almost blue from the strain of surgery. Machines seemed to be hooked to her from multiple directions. Yet, her face seemed welcoming, her eyes far less weak than one would have predicted.

"How are you feeling?" Jess' question came as she looked over the scene.

"Are they gone?" Roh's question jutted in sharp angles, a mismatch of an answer to her lover's question.

Jess looked around. "The nurses? Yeah they're gone, for now. But they'll probably be back in a few minutes."

"You gotta get me out of here." Roh's voice was even and unbending.

Jess shook her head. "There's no way. You're torn to shit! It's a miracle you're still alive." Jess could feel her control start to slip a bit as she thought back to holding her bleeding lover in her arms.

Roh's voice never wavered. "If I stay here, I'm dead. I was always supposed to avoid hospitals. Always. Now, the surgeons saw too much. They'll be working out details they shouldn't know. No one who worked on me will live through the night. If I'm lucky, they'll grab me, mend me, and force me to do my final job. They're not going to let me live."

Jess' mouth hung open. It was Regan who spoke up. "How do we even move you without killing you, Roh? You look like you're hooked up to every machine they've got." Regan gestured at the array of sensors and tubes attached to Roh.

Roh shook her head gently. "I don't need them. The doctors already know that, but there's no way they were going to stop monitoring me."

Regan and Jess spoke in unison: "Holy shit!"

"I'm not going to be running any time soon, but once they had me stable I could feel myself coming back out of sedation. At that point, I started healing."

Finally, Jess formed a full sentence. "That's not possible, Roh. That's so far beyond what's possible in modern medicine as to be laughable. We're talking science fiction here."

Rather than speak, Roh lifted an arm, and with her other arm slid her gown sleeve down. Her skin was marred, but just as she predicted, the wounds had closed. Jess started to wobble, and Regan caught her as her legs gave out from under her.

"Easy there, Buttercup," Regan helped her take two steps to a nearby seat. Then, she turned back to Roh. "They aren't going to let you leave." It wasn't even a question anymore. It was a statement.

"Nope."

"Once we unhook you, the machines are going to call the nurses. Can you walk?"

Roh frowned. "I don't think so. At least, not yet."

"I'll be right back," Regan said. "Can you keep Buttercup company? She's looking a few shades of green at the moment."

Roh smiled her affirmative and Regan took off.

"What's this 'Buttercup' business?" Roh asked, tease laced in her voice.

Jess slowly stood. "She knows it pisses me off, so she'll use it to get my attention. I swear to god, don't you dare pick it up."

They took a moment for their eyes to meet and for a smile to be shared between them.

"Fuck, Roh. You have no idea how good it is to see you alive," Jess didn't drop her gaze as she talked, instead she held it as if holding on for dear life.

Before she had time to hear Roh's response, Jess spun round to a sound of a whirlwind entering the ICU room. Regan was there with a wheelchair in hand.

"We have thirty seconds to get her into the elevator." Regan's voice strained at the words in a way that felt alien to anyone who knew her well. The tone catapulted Jess into action. Not knowing what to do, she tried to find lines she knew how to unhook and tore at tape and tube freeing what she could.

Roh, without hesitation, grabbed a whole handful of them all at once. "We don't have time." She pulled hard and ripped out as much as she could.

Seconds later, Regan and Jess helped Roh up and into the chair.

To Jess, everything felt saturated in adrenaline. She couldn't think clearly, she just automatically moved behind Regan, following her to the elevator she had found. Even when they were in it with the door closed, Jess dared not take too large of a breath.

The door dinged and opened onto the parking floor, requiring Regan to swipe a card to get access.

"They'd normally make us take the front door. This was the only thing I could think of." Regan explained as she pushed Roh forward. It took longer to find her car taking this exit, but few people were in this part of the parking area.

"Where are we going to go?" Roh's question came from her with the same even temperament most things did.

"First, to my car. Then we're going to start driving."

"Where to?" Jess asked, her brain kicking back into gear.

"We'll figure that out in the car."

A second later, Regan's car beeped as the doors unlocked. They helped Roh into the car, then set off down the road. Jess watched out the window from the back seat as Regan drove, all too conscious of the blood that hadn't quite dried under her.

The phone in Jess' pocket buzzed. "Good job. Twice. I owe you one." She stared at the message, quickly sympathising with Roh why she hated this man so much. She hadn't saved Roh because he'd ordered her to.

"Benjy is such an ass." Jess was tempted to just turn off her phone, but instead she spun it face down and held it against her leg.

Roh chuckled from the front seat. "That he is." Jess looked up at her, catching part of her reflection in the rearview mirror. Roh's colour was returning, bit by bit, to her cheeks. Jess felt thankful for small mercies.

"Can you eat?" It was Roh's voice. Jess hadn't realised that her attention had drifted. She looked up, and they were at the shops in a part of town she didn't know. She nodded in affirmative. "Can you get her a chicken sandwich and some juice?" Again, Roh, calm and collected, seemed to be handling things. Jess fought to understand what was happening.

"Where are we going?"

"We need to plan," Roh explained. "Regan has a place outside of the city that's a bit off the map. She said we could stay there for a day or two and figure out our next move. I flicked Benjar an update but didn't tell him where we'll be. He's going to use the info you gave him to see if we can start tracking these g-men a bit better. That should at least give us a heads up if they're coming our way."

Jess frowned. The information she'd given Benjar? Oh right, the hacking she'd done with Regan earlier. It seemed like a year ago. She was pretty sure she hadn't had any real sleep in at least a day and a half. The thought made her bone tired.

"We'll get you some food and then some rest."

Jess reached up and gently held Roh's shoulder. Roh turned back to hold her gaze. "You okay?"

"Am I okay? You've been through a meat grinder and the scalpel brigade, and you're asking me if I'm okay?"

"Yeah."

Jess just stared at her. "I'm not, really. Not until we figure out what's going on. Roh?"

"Hmm?"

"How are you not tense? You sound so relaxed."

Roh shrugged a bit, her head leaning to the side as if in thought. "Harder to make the jump if you're too tense."

Jess gave her a quizzical look in response, then slid her fingers in Roh's hair. She felt Roh lean into her and make a purring sound.

"You're fucking cute." Regan handed Roh the bag, then reached in and handed Jess a sandwich from it. "Eat up. We're going to need the brain food in half an hour."

RECHARGING

ROH

Roh sat on the couch and watched Regan and Jess give into frustration at their fruitless planning. There were too many unknowns. How can you fight something that you don't understand? How can you reason with shadows and spooks?

Jess looked back over the folder Roh had stolen, and again she looked confused. She had explained that too much of it was either basic vitals or written in some kind of code that she couldn't easily crack. She'd spread it out around her as they talked, but said she could tell pretty quickly that, unless she had a lucky guess with the cypher, it could take weeks or months to crack it. People with the right software could likely crack it faster, but to seek out help would put them in even more danger, Jess had explained.

Jess pointed at the header on one of the papers. "That said, I've seen this symbol before. Somewhere. Fuck, I can't remember, though." It didn't look like much to Roh, but she never really had a good memory for those things. Cities? Yes. Random drawings? Not so much.

"We need to take a break and recharge." Regan leaned back

and stared up at the ceiling. Roh felt the energy of the room noticeably shift from stressed to something a bit more sexual.

"Does recharge mean what I think it means?" Roh asked.

Regan looked over to Jess, then to Roh. "If you're up for it."

Roh looked down at the empty plate at her feet. An hour earlier, she had made herself a sandwich, against many Jess protests, to see if she was feeling well enough to move around and to test her coordination. She'd healed remarkably well. Some pains and aches still lingered, and she wasn't sure she wanted to give her body a full test on the rooftops, but she felt more like herself than she had when they'd arrived hours earlier.

The freerunner felt more cautious than anything. "I think so? Let's start slow and we'll see."

The two friends met with a practiced grace, their lips tender and familiar. The shock of the image pulled Roh in.

Her breath caught, but moments later her body tensed. It was Regan who broke the kiss. With it, she turned to face her. "On second thought," Reagan said, "I'm going to take a shower. I could use one. Take your time, it'll be a long one." Regan gently squeezed Roh's shoulder as she passed and headed to the bathroom.

As Roh turned to face Jess, she saw a look of concern in Jess' eyes. "Do you want to talk about it?" her lover asked.

Roh opened her mouth, then closed it. She'd always thought of herself as pretty sexually liberated. Sure, most of her girlfriends were monogamous. And sure, even when she'd have the odd friends-with-benefits, she mostly just played with one person at a time. She let the thoughts bounce around in her mind. Had she never really tested her comfort zones before?

Jess scooted closer, putting her hand in Roh's. "We don't have to talk now, but if you want to talk about it, I'm here."

Roh watched the look of pure care and concern on Jess'

face and wondered at how they seemingly had grown so close so quickly. If she hadn't known better, she would have said they'd been dating for months. Maybe more.

How had it all happened? How had she earned such affection from someone so different to her?

Acting on instinct, Roh reached up and pulled Jess into a kiss. Something in her wanted to read her lips as much as her face. To feel those feelings pass between them again. Just as she expected, Jess was at the ready to show her just how much Roh meant to her. It almost brought a tear to Roh's eye as she backed off the kiss and looked Jess in the face.

"Yeah, we can talk about it."

"Were you jealous?"

Roh thought. She let her body respond with its own answer as well. "I'm not sure what I felt. Maybe the need to protect?"

"To possess?" Jess added lightly, as if its own question. Roh stared at her lover's blushing face before she responded.

"Probably that, too."

Jess bit her lip before she spoke. "You already have me. If I'm honest, you have me so deeply, I can't see my life without you. When I thought I'd lost you, that was too much to bear. Nothing we do with Regan will change that. But I have to be honest. While I have no desire to risk what we have between us, I can't risk losing who I am in those feelings."

They let the silence settle in, each only searching the eyes of the other. Then Roh felt a hand touch her cheek gently, as if Jess were trying to communicate her feelings through just her fingers alone. The sensation was calming, though Roh's neck continued to hold all the same tension.

At last, Jess spoke again. "I love with a heart that, as much as possible, is wide open. I care. It lets me feel in ways that are difficult to explain. I can't do this with everyone, of course. There are plenty of people I've met and all they are is a quick hookup. They're just fun for a night and then we move on. They don't have the connection to me, nor I to them, that lets it be anything more.

But with some people, I bond. It's like friendship, lover, playmate, companion, you name it - all rolled up into one. Those relationships don't want to have any boundaries. Boundaries hurt them from flowing how they want to flow, which is something much more organic."

Roh felt a flash of insight cross her mind. "When you were asking if I wanted to have a threesome shortly after we met, you weren't talking about Regan, were you?"

Jess smiled. "That's... impressive. No, I wasn't. I was talking about Beth, who you might have met in the lab and the donut shop." Jess looked into Roh's face for a moment before she continued. "The people I'm close to, I'm close to. There's enough of me to..."

Jess' voice trailed off as Roh drew her thumb along Jess' bottom lip.

She studied Jess then. That sense of something vital within her always seemed to show through, even when she was her most worried or distracted. Even now, she could feel it coming off her and filling the space between them. Roh felt something stir in her heart as she looked at her.

An aching.

It was as if her heart had found itself in a cage by accident, and she wanted to be free. The thing that Jess had, Roh found herself wanting.

A moment later, Roh felt Jess' hand land on her chest over her heart. Roh felt desire course through her body. Something about this woman. It wasn't just that energy she couldn't quite understand. It was something else, too.

Jess leaned in and gently nibbled at Roh's ear lobe. Without pulling away, she whispered, "Regan will probably want to join in when she gets out of the shower. We can hold off, I just…" Again, Jess paused as Roh turned towards her, kissing her ear in return.

"Let her join."

"You sure?" Jess' voice was but a whisper, but this close to Roh it sent a chill through her.

Rather than answer, Roh pulled Jess tight against her, meeting lips and tongue with a single, fluid moan. Jess joined in with her own moan at the rush of sensation.

They kissed for a minute, then Jess pulled away, her face hot, her breath coming in heaves. "Fuck, Roh." She managed but two words before she attacked Roh's neck. The sharp pain/pleasure of her bite sent Roh. She quickly wrapped her arms around Jess and let her gnaw at her soft flesh. The moan that escaped Roh's lips had to have travelled down the hall because she heard its echo as it bounced back.

Jess pulled back and reached for Roh's top, a jumper Regan had let her borrow. As she pulled it over her head, Jess gasped.

There wasn't a single red wound anywhere on Roh's body. Seeing Jess' reaction reminded her of how exceedingly special her healing was. It was something she relied on, so much so it'd almost become second nature to her.

Jess reached up and ran her finger along the deep, thick scar on Roh's arm. Less than a day earlier she had been bleeding out from that and other gashes. Now, though heavily scarred, they looked more like ancient war wounds than freshly closed tears.

"How in the fuck?" Jess said in awe.

"We'll figure it out." Roh didn't mean to sound dismissive of her lover's distraction, but she was all too used to her own capacity for healing. Awe wasn't the kind of attention Roh was yearning for in the moment.

"What other things can you do?" Jess asked with what sounded like intellectual curiosity.

Roh was undistracted. "It's better if I show you."

Jess swore as Roh bit into her neck. Roh could feel her desire grow as her lover gave into her. She reached a hand up into Jess' hair and grabbed a fistful of it, holding her tight.

Leaning in, Roh let her voice be a demanding whisper. "As much as I love to spend the afternoon marking each other, I have something else for your mouth to do."

Jess whimpered at that. Roh kissed her, smiling into the kiss, then lifted herself up enough to pull down her jeans and underwear.

Roh had nearly closed her eyes after minutes of the hot oral affection when she spied Regan round the corner. As they locked eyes, Regan kept a respectful distance, her face a questioning look.

Roh simply nodded at her, not wanting to distract the all too lovely sensations Jess was able to produce.

21

COITUS INTERRUPTUS

JESS

One minute, Jess had her mouth gloriously filled with girl-cock without a care in the world. The next, she felt another pair of hands tugging up her borrowed skirt until it was past her hip. She tried her best to move to being on all fours while keeping Roh in her mouth, giving who she could only guess was Regan access to her bottom half.

Moaning on Roh's member was all she could do as she felt her panties get tugged down. Roh's hardness in her mouth and Roh's strength on her back sent warm heat between her legs. A moment later, she realised that not only did she have a better angle on Roh, Regan had a better angle on her.

The moment Regan pushed inside of her, Jess evaporated into a world of sensation. Being surrounded by people she cared about, having the kind of sex she wanted - no, needed - to have, sent hot chills through her. It took the sensation of Roh rubbing her head for Jess to be aware of the sounds she was making.

Jess took Roh as deeply as she could, fighting off the tears and giving herself over to being fully fucked in both ends. She moaned again as she felt Roh tense. She watched her lover's hands claw at her legs rather than giving into the temptation to push Jess down further.

As Jess tasted Roh's release in her mouth, her own warmth doubled in her belly. Without a word, Roh lifted her head up, letting her gasp briefly before covering Jess' lips with her own. Her tongue was hot and needy, drinking in both Jess and herself. Feeling Roh's affection kept that feeling of fullness growing.

She pulled back from Roh, her eyes a frown of concentration.

"More. More. More." Jess' voice was pleading, her need raw for everyone in the room.

"I'm giving it all she's got, capt'n," Regan replied, sounding more than a little out of breath.

Jess sighed loudly and then did the first thing that came to mind - she leaned over and bit Roh hard. The effect focused her mind, letting her give into Regan and finally crest where the tension had been building.

A minute later all three of them had collapsed to the floor, howling laughing. "Holy shit, you bit the fuck out of my arm." Roh showed her lovers proudly. "I'm not going to be mad if that leaves a mark."

Jess turned to Regan, who was pulling off her strap. "You always have to bring out the big toys whenever I'm around, don't you?"

Regan, wiping a tear from her eye, could only nod in response. "Oh I have all sorts of big toys for you, including ones that will leave you little more than a puddle on the floor."

Jess looked over at the comically large dildo. "Roh, you feel like giving it a go?"

"Ha! Fuck no. I'd have to practise for months to take that!" Roh was still laughing, her eyes wide.

"What if we found something a bit more to your liking?" Jess' voice took on a purr as she fixed her eyes on Roh.

"What's Regan going to do, watch?" Roh's voice had a bit of a tease to it, as if she wanted to make Regan watch.

Regan's grin was infectious. "Oh I have a better idea." With that, Regan laid down on the floor, her head pointed towards Roh. "Come on over."

"Ooooh," Jess smiled. "Give us a minute to find one she can take?"

"Don't take too long, I don't want to cool off."

Jess grabbed Roh's hand and pulled her to the office down the hall.

Roh cackled immediately as she entered the room. "That is the largest dildo collection I have ever seen!"

Staring at them from a large curio cabinet was a wide variety of dildos. Different colours, shapes. Some large and other small, shaped for other happy orifices. In the back, there stood a whole collection of the alien variety.

"We better pick something quickly. How's this one?" Jess pointed to one in the front middle of the cabinet.

"That'll work."

The two of them giggled like school girls on their way back to the den, Jess holding something that look like it came from a tall, purple tentacle monster.

"We're ready," Jess exclaimed. She pulled the strap tight and fitted the dildo into it.

Regan clapped her hands, then opened her arms in a warm gesture aimed at Roh. Roh obliged and crawled over her until she'd nestled into a sixty-nine position that fit their body lengths.

Jess smiled as she watched, eager to see just how distracted she could keep Roh. She knew all too well that Regan could keep Roh on edge for as long as possible. Beautiful, delicious torture.

Jess smiled again as she remembered that every drawer in this house, except those in the kitchen, all had condoms and lube. At least in the kitchen, some of the drawers had utensils in them.

She fitted on what she needed and ran her hands over the roundness of Roh's ass. God, Jess thought, she really was distractingly hot. The muscles alone almost made Jess lose concentration a second time.

It was Roh's moan that brought her back to the present moment. Regan was already working her magic.

"Oh, I see," Jess teased. "You think you're moaning now, just you wait." It took Jess a moment to get into position, careful not to pinch any of Regan's hair under her knees. Jess did secretly wonder how well Roh could handle being penetrated while being pleasured. Jess knew from her early years that blood flow could be a bit stingy.

The scientist put her strap to work, coaxing it into Roh, who rolled her back and let out something guttural in response. The motion so hypnotised Jess, she almost forgot was she was doing. She managed to steady herself and hold on, pushing the strap the rest of the way home.

A flash of images ran through her mind. A hospital smell. Men walking into her room. Men who didn't look like doctors.

Roh moaned again, though this time it sounded different. "Jess?"

Jess tried to snap out of it, not know how much time had passed. The feeling of the images lingered.

"Are you going to finish me?" Roh asked, her voice laced with annoyance. Jess looked down to see she was still inside her lover.

"I think I should sit down," Jess said, pulling out. The other two untangled and turned to her with concerned expressions.

"You okay, babe?" Roh said, her face glistening with juices.

"I'm really not. How long was I not moving?"

Roh took an arm and rubbed at her mouth. "Not more than maybe 30 seconds? I was a bit distracted."

"I don't remember any of it," Jess admitted.

"What?" Regan crawled over to her and held her face. "Do you feel sick? Headache? Numbness on one side of the body?"

"It's nothing, I just..." Jess wasn't really sure what to say. She'd had distracted moments before, but never during sex.

She sat back against the couch and looked at them. Both Regan and Roh stared back at her, their faces drawn tight with concern.

"When was the last time you slept?" Roh asked her, taking her hand. Her lover's touch felt soft, despite the callouses on her hands. Jess could only shake her head.

With that, Regan showed them to a bed and promised they could sleep as long as necessary. Or, until the house got raided by nameless government entities. Regan deigned to even add "pleasant dreams" to the end.

"I'm going to kill her," Jess said, her eyes already heavy with sleep.

"Can you kill her after we wake up?" Roh wrapped herself around Jess, and the two fell fast asleep.

———

Jess slept the syrupy sleep of the rest-starved, her dreams a mess of images, feelings, anxieties, and desires. The mess of images formed into their own dream. A body, on the ground, its head turned towards the grass, appeared ahead of her in the haze.

As Jess reached down to touch the body, its head swivelled towards her in an inhumanly doll-like motion. Its face, porcelain and lifeless in its stillness, moved to stare at Jess.

"Look at you wasting your life away," the doll chided. "You should be settled down now. When are you going to get married?"

"There's nothing wrong with pleasure," Jess retorted. "I don't have to settle down. I'm allowed to be free."

"Being allowed to do something is just the first step. You should choose to do what's best."

"And what is that?" Jess sneered.

"If you don't wake up to what's available in the world around you, you'll lose it." The doll cackled in an eerie echo, that went on and on.

22

FUGUE STATES

ROH

Jess moaned in her sleep as Roh tried to shake her awake. She mumbled something about a laughing doll that won't get the last laugh, but she refused every attempt to break from whatever nightmare she'd found herself in.

Roh didn't have a choice. She hefted Jess off the bed.

"Ok, sleeping beauty. You need food in you."

With a gymnast's grace, she carried her into the living room and set her down on the sofa, making sure her head rested peacefully on the pillow.

"If I can't wake you, the smells will."

After Roh stood, Regan came up to her, close enough to whisper. "Has she told you about what causes those spells?"

Roh shook her head.

"I'll let her tell you. We have to watch her. Most of the time they're harmless. Luckily, if they happen when she's driving, she can still manage to drive somewhere, even if it's not where she meant to go." Regan smiled at that, but Roh wasn't sure if she wanted to.

Jess stirred beneath her, and Roh instinctively squatted down. "Hey sleepyhead."

Jess opened her eyes. "What time is it?"

"Not morning," Roh replied. "We've got food if you're hungry."

"Starving." Jess rallied and pulled herself into a sitting position.

"You had me worried last night," Roh admitted. "I thought you had a stroke or something."

"Sorry, I shouldn't have pushed for a second round. I knew I was about to pass out." Jess slowly shook her head. "I feel like I got hit by a DC-10."

"That's rather specific," Roh said as she cracked a smile.

"Well, you see it's larger than a… never mind." Jess looked over to Regan, then back to Roh. "What's for breakfast? I smell something of the bacon variety."

"Yeah, she's awake enough, let's go." With that, Roh pulled Jess to her feet and they made their way to the kitchen.

Regan's kitchen was a royal affair. Roh didn't recognise most of it, but the cabinets and appliances looked like the kind you'd see in the most expensive parts of town. Flat magic cooking surfaces coated in something that seemed to stay immaculately clean, that is, unless Regan was just that clean. But no human actually was. Roh suspected she had better things to do.

The magic continued to the cabinetry, which seemed to pull and turn and silently close, all in some kind of overly expensive dance. Regan took a minute to select the perfect plates for the meal, and Roh quickly stepped over to help her plate up and get the food to the table.

"Sorry, my chef is out today." Regan chuckled. From how she said it, Roh thought there was much more to the story. "Silverware is over there, if you'd be the hot thing I know you to be and fetch some for us."

Jess watched Roh blush an almost imperceptible amount as she grabbed silverware from the drawer.

As they ate, Regan spoke in her professional voice, "You two have work to do today. I've got to run to the office, but I'll be back later."

"Wait, you're going into the office, won't that be a huge risk?" Jess frowned at her.

"I hear what you're saying, but if I'm not safe in a government building where there are a hundred witnesses, I'm going to feel like a fugitive."

"Won't they just flash their badge?" Roh asked, spinning her fork around with particular dexterity.

Regan looked pensive. "Do we actually think they really are g-men? Are we dealing with some government agency that outranks the judicial office?"

Jess and Roh looked at each other and shrugged. Roh spoke first, "It's possible. They never told me anything, but that doesn't mean they aren't in some politician's back pocket."

Regan shook her head. "If they actually are some kind of shadow government agency, then I want to know who they are. I want to know who we're dealing with. Does this guy you're working with know anything?"

"Benjar?" Roh asked.

"That's the one. Does he know anything about them?"

"He does owe me one," Roh looked down at her food and stabbed at it. "If he doesn't know anything, then he's been leading me on this whole time."

"Which, having met him, sounds more than a little possible," Jess added.

"We've tried what we can. Benjar needs to cough up if he's got it. The records were a bust, at least so far. I can pull the strings that I have. Talk to politicians, do a bit of leaning. But they need to see my face for this to work best, I'm afraid. Weasels will weasel unless they can smell a real predator."

Roh and Jess both giggled at that. Roh could only imagine what Regan would be like when she put her mind to it.

After breakfast had finished, Regan picked up the dishes and was out the door with few words.

"How are you feeling?" Roh asked as they made their way back to the living room.

"It was nothing. It was just," Jess began and then stopped. "What?"

"Regan mentioned sometimes you have spells."

"Like magic?" Jess snickered.

"You know what I mean."

"They're nothing. I've had them since I was a teen. Kind of like being really focused on something, so focused that I lose myself in it."

"Or blank out."

"Yeah, or blank out," Jess admitted.

"I heard one time about a husband who would get occasional fugue states. Said he left his wife during one of them and woke up with a strange woman."

Jess chucked. "You worried I'm going to drive off and wake up with strange women?"

"From what I can tell, you're already pretty good at finding strange women without any help." Roh laughed, running her fingers through Jess' hair. Suddenly, the couch felt a little small.

Jess turned slightly towards her but kept her head in petting range. "What about you? How are you feeling after yesterday?"

"I'm... okay, I think. It was fun."

"But not something you'd make a regular habit of?"

Roh when silent for a moment, her petting slowed but didn't stop. "I'm not sure. It's one thing to focus on someone and put your energy into them. It's something else to find ways to share someone. It's a different muscle, one I'm not sure I have in large quantities."

"Because the muscle needs to be built up or because you'd rather not work that muscle?" Jess asked.

"Probably more the former than the latter," Roh replied.

With the ease of having done the move hundreds of times, Jess rounded and spun a leg over Roh, sitting up in her lap. "You know, you don't have to push it if you're not comfortable. I have my needs, but there are different ways to work that. We could do it separately or together."

"You make it sound like I'm being taken into your equation," Roh said, giving her a smile.

"If only you knew how much of that equation you were part of." At that, Jess' voice trailed off. She leaned in and kissed Roh's neck and then sat back. "You just reminded me of something."

"Tell me."

"Regan was teasing me about the Bonobo Devices, too. Said they needed to do more."

"Uh oh, am I about to lose you to that inventor brain of yours?" Roh asked.

Jess leaned in and planted a kiss on Roh's lips, then pulled away. "Maybe."

"Do you think it'll help us get out of this mess?"

Jess tilted her head. "Now that is an excellent question."

"Would you like to get naughty first?" Roh ask, her grin wicked and charming.

"You do make it tempting, but I'll have to take a rain check. Cuddles, though? I'm all in for cuddles."

Roh's grin held. "Cuddles sound excellent."

They adjusted their position on the couch until Roh was spooning Jess, resting their heads against the side of the sofa.

"This is nice," Roh said, nuzzling her face against the back of Jess' neck. She could tell Jess was already lost to whatever was happening in her head, so she pulled her tighter. Something about how much Jess loved, both loving her friends and partners, but also how much she got into her work, made Roh feel fuzzy and warm.

Just as Roh was about to lightly drift off to sleep, she heard Jess mumble something.

"What was that?" Roh asked quietly.

"Do you think people will let us into their emotions?"

Roh moaned lightly as she pressed her face against Jess. "I don't know. I guess it depends on what you have in mind."

"What if we could show them everything they couldn't see?" Jess asked the room and seemingly the audience of her peers in her head.

"What do you mean, babe?" Roh let out the question, not really expecting an answer.

"So many of our emotions are jumbled mess like a burrito order. Sure, you can pick the onions out, but can you really unmix the refried beans, salsa, and sour cream once that's all mixed together? We're like a purée up in there."

Roh tried her best to stifle her giggles but found herself progressively failing. "God, you are cute as fuck, but sometimes I haven't a clue what you're talking about."

Jess continued as if she hadn't heard. "Emotions are like monodic functions, with folds that occur out of sight until we get a result that's hidden its steps."

Roh sighed a little. "I officially have zero idea what you're talking about."

Jess turned to her then. "Emotions. They pop out of us, but they're a collection of so many processes we can't see. Why do we get jealous or angry? We have to figure it out. We can feel the emotion, we can feel it in our bones, in our belly, in our very scalp, but how was that emotion formed? It didn't come from nothing. Something, or somethings, made it. We aren't transparent at all. We're opaque, even to ourselves. I mean, maybe some nun in a cave has cracked the code. The rest of us? Hell, the cave doesn't have any lights. We're just stumbling in the dark hoping to happen on a good therapist to explain something to us and maybe they get it right."

"I think I managed to follow some of that. If I'm being optimistic."

Jess kissed her absent-mindedly on the cheek. "We have our intuition, and it can be helpful. But, imagine. Wouldn't it be better to actually know where an emotion really came from? When we have an intuition, to know how we know it so we know how much we can trust it?"

"How would we know that?" Roh asked, even more curious now that it was starting to click what Jess was going on about.

"There's a long-held theory in meditation circles that thoughts and emotions have multiple stages. That there are stages most people never notice because they're just outside of conscious thought. Maybe we can find them? Maybe we can figure out in the brain where they're happening and what they mean. If we can do that, we can possibly form a better, more complete picture of your inner world for you."

"If you can do that, babe, you deserve a medal." Roh returned the kiss and looked at her lover. Pride ran along her skin as she watched her brain work. She reached up, not able to contain herself, and gently stroked Jess' cheek.

Jess turned to her then, finally locking eyes with her. "I think I have my problem to solve."

"It sounds like you do. Hopefully it helps us, too" Roh said.

"That I'm not sure if it will, but even if it doesn't help us, maybe it'll help other people."

Roh couldn't help herself. Her heart swelled at the idea

that Jess could be thinking about people outside of herself when they were still in danger. To Roh, danger was always there, in some amount. A life lived without risk wasn't actually possible. Even if you lived a life inside your house, you'd risk your health through inactivity. The trick, she'd noticed, was not letting yourself become possessed by the risks in your life. To look outside of them. At least, she thought, it's what she tried to do on a good day. Still, this was all in theory and theory never seemed to bring home rent money.

Roh cleared her throat. "Do you think being more aware of feelings would improve how people treated each other? I mean, even if you did, how are you going to get people to wear it? Plenty of people think they already have the right of it. They wouldn't believe you if you told them they were missing so much."

She wanted to be supportive, but her gut was telling her there were more than a few kinks to work out in the plan.

Roh felt fingers at her cheeks, gently stroking them. Roh turned to her, now aware she'd looked away.

"The moment someone famous talks about how using it saved them from making a really bad decision, we'll have people asking what they are. It feels mean to say it, but we're like a school of fish. If one of us turns and seems to know what they're doing, we tend to follow."

"Especially if that fish happens to be particularly famous." Roh chuckled, and she shook Jess with the force of it.

Jess signed and shrugged as best she could in the cuddle. "Exactly."

"I never did anything like that. I just did jobs. Other people were playing the game."

Jess nuzzled in. "Other people are always playing the game. I play as much as I need to, but I try not to play any more than that. I love my work. When it comes down to it. That's what I want to do, and I play the game enough to keep doing it."

"What would you do if you didn't have to?"

Jess shrugged again. "Honestly, I don't believe in any job that doesn't have some kind of paying the piper. Everything is a trade. Everywhere takes their pound of flesh."

Roh's voice dropped. "Speaking of pounding flesh."

Jess kissed her on the cheek. "I owe you one and trust me that I appreciated how you handled that. I don't always take the best care, let's say. That you stepped up meant a lot."

"Do you have those spells often?" Roh asked, looking away to not seem too eager. She had spent a part of the morning wondering how much danger this woman she was falling for was to herself.

"I," Jess began, then paused. She sighed, as she looked in Roh's eyes. "I probably should tell you about them. Yeah," Jess said as if psyching herself up.

Roh studied her. She'd never really seen her lover lose her confidence. "If you don't want to talk about it…"

"It's not that. It's just not easy to talk about. My spells, these fugues, they got worse in my twenties, right after someone I trusted beat the shit out of me. They were so angry. I'd never seen them like that before. Something about… Something set them off. It was bad. I had to go to the hospital."

The tenderness rose through Roh's chest. She watched as Jess' eyes brimmed with tears. "Holy shit, babe. I'm so sorry."

"After that, they got worse. A lot worse. At first, I felt self-conscious about them, then I guess I just started to accept them. Mostly they're harmless. Sometimes, I even get a good idea from them."

Roh rubbed at her nose absentmindedly. "Don't take this the wrong way, but I'm surprised you don't have someone drive you around."

"You aren't the first person to suggest that. Honestly, most of the time it's a good thing. It helps me fall into my work, to go deep with it, and see problems in a way that'd be hard to do otherwise. Sure, I annoy my friends at parties, but they still put up with me. Hell, I made it this far."

Roh ran her fingers through Jess' hair and kept silent. Then, she spoke up, "If you want, you can do it now."

Roh felt Jess squeeze her tightly. "I'd rather be here with you."

Roh looked at her then. Jess' eyes were bright and full of life, and more than that, full of something that felt like gratitude. It made her relax into the snuggle. There would no doubt be things to work through, and few, if any, would get solved in a few minutes. Instead, she changed topics. "We should check in with Benjy. As fun as staying here is, and no doubt more fun awaits when Regan gets back, I'd feel a bit better being closer to the city. It'd make it easier for me to keep us safe."

"I know, babe. This was really only meant to be a temporary solution. Do you think we can get back without them catching us?" While Jess asked the question, she sat up and moved her hands to Roh, gently lifting her sleeves. "That's fucking something. I wish I had any idea what they'd done to you. Might help us know what we're dealing with."

Roh's wounds were scars now, as if she'd healed for months. Even Roh knew that wasn't humanly possible, and yet she'd grown used it.

"I wonder why the scars don't heal?" Jess said to herself, gently running a finger over one. Roh patiently let her do it. "I guess scars are like that. Though don't ever fully heal. We wear them, whether they're on the outside or the inside."

Roh purred a little. "Perhaps, but if you keep rubbing me like that, you might start warming me up, and I thought you wanted to snuggle."

"Can I work? Here, with you, I mean?"

Roh nodded. "I already said that was okay, if you wanted to."

"I just want to be close to you, but my mind is running ahead and I need to give it something to do."

Jess went off and pillaged a few notebooks from Regan's stash and a wide selection of pens. She sat down with her back to the couch as she opened the first one, carefully selecting a pen from the ones she'd found.

"Is it okay if I touch you?" Roh asked, tentatively.

"Absolutely." Jess gave her a warm smile then turned back to the notebook. Soon enough, the first page was filled with complete gibberish, at least to Roh's eyes. Without much to hold her attention, Roh let her own thoughts roam before she picked up her phone. She typed out a message to Benjar with one hand while her other hand was busy stroking Jess' hair.

A minute later, Roh's phone buzzed. There were routes back that were open. They just needed a car.

Then, another text. Regan. *"You're hot fun. When all this blows over, consider yourself invited."*

Roh chuckled.

"Did Regan ask if you wanted in on the next orgy?" Jess asked, her eyes still locked on her arcane scribbles.

"Good guess, how'd you know?"

"She tends to do that with people she likes. And she definitely sounded like she liked what you were doing to her."

"Is she always like that?" Roh asked, her voice a bit unsteady as to how to ask in a way that wouldn't offend Jess.

"For as long as I've known her." With that, Jess tore out a notebook page with a fierce finality and laid it beside two other pages.

Roh looked over at them, but it was hopeless. "Figuring anything out?"

Jess didn't respond.

"Babe?"

"Oh sorry, didn't hear you. Look, look." Whatever Jess said next made absolutely no sense. It was like English had been replaced by some kind of translator that only output alien.

"Slow down. I don't understand a word you said." Then, Roh froze. Without a sound, she gently moved her finger to lightly cover Jess' lips. "Something's wrong. Let me see if I can figure out what it is."

They sat in silence. Nothing.

Then, a knock at the door. Their eyes went as big as saucers.

They crept on tip toes to the door, Roh in the front, as she silently hoped the front door had a peephole. It did.

She looked, and her eyes grew wider. It was Jess' friend from the lab and the bar. She turned to Jess and mouthed "why is your friend here?"

Jess pushed past her and looked through the peephole.

23

OLD FRIENDS

JESS

Sure enough, Beth was outside. And she looked scared shitless.

The need to run assaulted Jess' senses. Everything about this was wrong. Sure, Beth knew where Regan's place was. They'd partied together plenty of times. But this was definitely not that. This was Beth looking like her life was in danger.

Everything about it felt like a trap, even to Jess. They should run. Don't fall into the trap. That was the whole point of recognising it was a trap, so you could step around it. Avoid it. Not fucking fall into it.

And yet.

One of her dearest friends was standing on the porch, looking like she was about to explode.

A cold chill rand down Jess, and despite all the voice screaming in her head, she slowly opened the door.

"Beth?"

She looked like her knees were barely holding her up.

"Don't move," she said, slowly lifting a hand to point at the camera at chest height. "They know you're both here. If you don't come with me, they're not going to let me live." Every word cracked under the weight of the meaning behind them.

"We need to get our stuff," Jess tried.

"Come as you are. Don't even bother putting on shoes. Just come out with me and don't make any quick movements."

"Reach into the drawer and fetch me Regan's backup Bonobo," Jess said, without turning away from Beth. She heard Roh move behind her, then hand her the device. She put it on as she walked towards Beth slowly.

Once she was within arm's reach, she stopped. "Lead the way."

Jess could feel Roh tense behind her. The tension lingered, but never was voiced. The three of them set off to Beth's car, parked on the street a house down.

"Are you okay to drive?"

"I don't know, but they didn't give me much choice."

Jess opened her mouth to ask who, but what was the point. She already knew. Of course, they'd get around being tracked. Of course, they'd evade Benjar's notice. Of course. Jess rolled her eyes that trying to outsmart bad guys in reality was decidedly harder than in the movies. They had a lot more practice, after all.

All three got into the car, with Jess and Roh letting Beth drive from the front while they climbed into the back.

Roh tapped Jess on the leg as the car left the curb. She mouthed, *why didn't they just kill us?*

Jess shook her head. She didn't know either. They could have strapped Beth with explosives and made quick, albeit very obvious, work of it. She didn't dare ask, but she could imagine that wouldn't be something Roh would have bounced back from.

The thought sent a shiver through her, and she reached out and held Roh's hand.

Roh mouthed again, *I'm with you.*

Jess wanted to reply 'for now', but she held it in. What good was pouring ice water on an already chilly situation? She had no idea what these g-men wanted, especially out of her, but she doubted they'd keep them together.

She looked up at Beth and felt sadness fill her. She didn't ask for this. Jess hadn't, either, in all honesty, but she'd jumped in with both feet once she had a chance to help Roh. Beth? Beth hadn't done anything but be at the wrong place at the wrong time and be friends with the wrong person. A bystander by any definition. Collateral damage.

Jess shivered at the thought.

She reached up and gently ran her fingers in Beth's hair, something she'd done hundreds of times before. An act that would be considered far too intimate for most friends, but something that'd developed to help calm each other. That and lewd jokes. Jess knew it was a long shot to try to calm her down. Even if the thought was appreciated, Beth was likely at her wits end.

With her other hand, she reached over to Roh. Even if the three of them didn't make it out of what was about to happen in one piece, at least they had this moment. For whatever that was worth. Jess internally shook her head. It was worth something. To be here with her lover and her dear friend to face what could be the most awful experience in her life - which was saying something.

However brief this ride was, Jess was going to treasure this moment of calm.

Jess looked over to Roh and tried her best to smile, then looked back to Beth. Again, her heart went out to her.

She thought back to their time in uni together. She'd met Beth a couple of years after Regan. Beth was never as wild as Regan was, preferring the lab to partying late into the night.

More than once Jess felt that the two of them gave her the full uni experience. Deep in the science and deep in the… well, multiple ways of going deep.

If anything happened to Beth, Jess knew she'd never be able to forgive herself.

How hard they fought together for those early grants. How hard they worked for the results that became papers that became more grants. Then the chance to get picked up and build an industrial lab. The Bonobo idea had been hers, but without Beth it would have been a shadow of what it had become.

How many times had Beth saved her in big and little ways? Reminded her of that important meeting so that she wouldn't space on it? Warned her by pointing out red flags in someone she was interested in? Beth never tried to have Jess for herself. It was never like that. She was always content to be a friend, to have occasional fun, but never be possessive.

Jess knew how rare friends like that were.

She'd worked hard, but she knew she'd gotten lucky. While so many people who showed themselves not to be friends when the pressure was on, she managed to find some who stuck around. Somewhere along the way, some dear people picked her out and said "You!" and didn't let her go. She felt so much gratitude for that.

She looked over at Roh and wondered again what they'd done to her. The healing was impossible, far beyond anything she'd ever seen in biochemical engineering. Far beyond the limits of any biotech she'd ever touched. Cells just didn't work like that. Cells got damaged and anything that said they could be repaired overnight was, as her academic advisor once said, something that should ping her "bullshit detector".

Roh wasn't bullshit. Not in her manner, not in her attitude, not in her affection, and certainly not in her ability to heal. How the fuck any of this was possible, Jess hadn't a clue.

Were they going to torture her? Put her healing to the test?

The thought of Roh being tortured turned Jess' stomach. She'd already seen enough. The barbed wire and the hospital. The waiting. The running.

———

Jess didn't open her mouth. Instead, she let herself fall into her thoughts. The car disappeared, though the sensation at her fingertips remained. She was going to solve the puzzle of how to keep everyone safe. If she could, she was going to manage it.

What could she trade that would be valuable enough to let the three of them go?

24

BELLY OF THE BEAST

ROH

Roh watched Jess fall into her trance, then looked ahead. She already knew where they were going. There wasn't any reason to ask. It was like that with Jess, too. She didn't have to ask her why she picked now to check out. She knew. Jess was trying to solve how to get them out of this mess. That's just how she was.

Roh already knew there was no bargaining with these people. They were the ones that made the bargains. When you're the juggernaut, none of the measly humans are going to have any leverage on you. Anyone who tries, and happens to get in the way, will just be crushed under heel.

"...for her."

It was Beth. The first words she'd uttered since getting in the car. Roh had been too lost in her own thoughts to catch them.

"What was that?" she asked.

"You need to watch out for her. She can't take stresses like this. Boardrooms are mostly okay, though she'll kill herself to prep for each one. But this? This is too much. She's going to push herself until she breaks."

Roh looked back at Jess, Beth's words ringing in her ears. How was she going to protect Jess?

"She's actually kind of fragile. I'm only saying this to you now because I don't think she can hear me."

Roh just nodded.

"Please." Beth's voice had taken on something new. A hurt pleaded. "I know you're special. Please." Beth's eyes sought her in the rearview mirror, held her gaze, and then returned to the road. With that, she went silent.

Roh didn't know what to say. She wasn't some kind of superhero. Sure, she didn't need as much sleep as other folks. Sure, she healed quickly. She couldn't fly. She didn't have eye lasers. She couldn't walk through walls or turn invisible. She was just a human. Yes, genetically modified likely, and modified in who knows how many other ways. She wasn't special, though. Not in the way Jess would need her to be.

Fragile.

Roh looked back at Jess, her face a mask of deep concentration. Her brow a permanent furrow. It took an act of will for Roh to not reach over and smooth it.

The route they were taking felt ominous. Another few turns, and they'd be back to the facility she'd escaped from. A place she sure as hell never wanted to go back to.

The car took a left, then a right, then pulled into an area under the facility. Beth drove them up to the doors marked Shipments. Men were already waiting for them.

For half a second, Roh thought through every possible means to escape, but they all ended with someone getting hurt. They had made the snare, and Roh knew better than to pull on it until she bled.

Even still, they grabbed her arms.

"I'm not going anywhere. You've got me. I'm not going to run." Roh looked over at Jess. She was still in a nearly catatonic state. They'd managed to get her into a wheelchair and were rolling her towards the entrance. "What are you going to do to her?"

"You should have thought of that before you tried to run," the suit beside her with crushing hand strength sneered in her ear. His voice roiled like an unruly cur, as if he was all too used to fighting for his corporate scraps. Roh didn't find him intimidating in the least.

She let them drag her inside as she studied the walls and the floor. It was just like she remembered it. She chanced a glance around, but they'd already turned Jess in another direction. Beth was nowhere to be found.

Her fate, it seemed, awaited just ahead.

WAKING NIGHTMARE

JESS

Jess awoke from her meditative state only to see that she was in a building she knew all too well. She screamed the loudest she'd ever screamed in her life.

THEY ACT AS A PRISM

ROH

Roh jerked hard against their grip as she heard her lover's voice echo from far down the hall. She considered biting them hard enough they'd let her go. The thought must have been too loud because one of the men turned to her.

"You're not getting out of here a second time." The words left his mouth with a calm, confident finality, as if he had no reason to lie.

Roh cursed to herself. They should have kept moving. Should have lived light and not been anywhere predictable. Should have. Lots of should's and nothing she could do about it now. Now, they were prisoners in every sense of the word.

Every muscle in Roh ached. They'd walked into this place willingly. To have their freedoms stripped from them willingly. The walls felt like they were closing in on her.

They pulled her down a hall and into an open door with a chair that looked like it would be right at home in a dentist's office. Oh fuck no.

"Look, I don't really think now is the time to check my oral hygiene," Roh quipped.

"Get in it and shut up," the man to her left barked. She glanced around the room for a weapon, anything to defend herself, but at least at a glance there were no dentist tools or otherwise in easy reach. The man, impatient, gave her an unhelpful push.

She begrudgingly fell into the chair, shooting a glance at the man who pushed her. He was just like all the others. She watched as a panel slid over her head and down in front of her.

"Oh nice, I get television. You didn't have to." Roh said, her voice mechanical and dry.

A doctor walked in, or at least, someone dressed like a doctor. Roh could only assume his profession. Something about him made Roh pale instantly.

"I see we're in high spirits," he said, looking through his tablet then up at her. "Ahh Roh. I'm surprised you kept that name. Apologies for misspelling it, Greek isn't my first language."

Each word was like an icicle dropping from the ceiling into her head. She knew this man, though every attempt to remember who he was failed her.

This man. This ice beast of a man. He reached out and dragged his thumb across the edge of her eye, catching a drop.

"A touching reunion, I see." The words drummed at her harder now.

Why was she crying? Why the fuck did this man have any control over her whatsoever? The thought struck her and vanished as quickly, leaving her stinging like a slap in the face.

"Well, we must move along, see. The day's precious hours are short. Shall we begin?" He chuckled to himself, then. "Oh, you needn't answer that. You already know what's about to happen."

Roh had no idea.

"I heard you'd been quite a sore spot of trouble lately. You shouldn't do that, you know. You were always going to end up back here when we wanted you."

Again, more icicles. Absolutely fuck this guy and the thousand horses he rode in on. Roh craned her neck, but it did little to calm the headache that rapidly grew behind her temples.

"You know, when you pulled that stunt the other day, I was worried you might actually kill yourself. Came close didn't you?"

Roh felt her vision darken at the sides. She didn't remember them injecting her with anything, but she could swear she'd been drugged.

He sat the tablet to the side and took a step closer to her, locking eyes with her. "There we go, I think we're just about in sync now."

The pounding in Roh's head grew exponentially. Surely someone was using a jackhammer nearby.

"You know it hurts less if you don't fight it."

Fight what?! Roh wanted to scream, but she couldn't find her voice.

"Let's begin." He raised his hand, as if conducting an invisible orchestra. Roh's eyes, now half-lidded in the pain and darkening vision, only made him out as a colourless blob in motion. His voice, though, was crystal clear to her eyes despite the cacophony in her other sense. He cleared his throat.

"When the sunlight strikes raindrops in the air..." Each word felt like ice shattering in her mind. The darkening tunnel closed, leaving her in darkness.

A moment later, she heard her voice, as if disembodied. "They act as a prism and form a rainbow."

Roh watched as her vision disintegrated, even the blacks became an array of separate colours. Then, a grid, a matrix of colours, stretched across her vision. A grid that had always been there, she recognised it, but it always sat just outside of her attention. The whites of the room returned first, but the white was no longer white. It danced like a million pixels rotating in hue, a field of noise where once was a single shade. Had the world always felt like this, but her mind had ignored it?

Shapes also returned, but each edge of each shape glowed. Had she been of the mind to see or feel things like a mystic, she might have felt like this was a mystical experience. Instead, it felt like someone peeling away at her mind, removing a bandage that had been trying its best to hold everything together.

Someone spoke, but she couldn't make out what they had said. *Odd*, Roh thought. Her ears a moment ago had been so clear. Now, she felt underwater. She strained to make out a single word she could understand. Instead, the sound seemed to cause ripples in her field of vision. She knew there was a word for this. Jess would probably know it.

Jess.

How was she going to protect her, now?

She willed her body to move. It refused. She willed her jaw to loosen and her tongue to help her speak. Neither budged. Fuck these disobedient organs.

She felt it then, starting from somewhere inside her head and then spreading out, a warmth. Wherever it spread seemed to relax.

This she instinctively fought. No good ever came from sedation, but she couldn't reach out and stop it. It was just there, inside her. Stretching through her. Filling her.

Making her pliable.

She fucking hated it.

She knew she was still in there. This effect wasn't her. Despite herself, though, she found she liked it. Which made her even more angry. She tried to ferret this part of her around

in her brain, to keep it safe from this numbing syrup that tried
to take her over.

She was still here.

She was still going to fight.

She was still...

UNWELCOME MEMORIES

JESS

Jess knew she was back in her own head. There were sounds around her. People shuffling about. She, however, was in her place.

She was also in this place. She knew it. It was all too easy to remember the smell, the decorations - which oddly hadn't changed much - and the layout. She'd spent time here recovering, after all. One gets an awful lot of time to memorise useless details when one has nothing to do.

Being twenty-four was years ago. An eon ago. But now, it felt like only moments had passed. Jess felt the fear of it. Every corner of her body was caked in sweat. That discomfort was nothing compared to the pain and shock, though.

How it happened had been a blur. The months of planning to get a date for her surgery. Her early successes as a specialist in medical engineering. All her money going to pay for something she'd dreamed of. She remembered that. Then, that asshole, her ex. Something about the operation had set them off. She'd been bullied before, but never like this. Her brain had blocked out what they'd done, only she remembered lying in a crumpled heap clutching her mess of a sex organ. They'd beaten her, beaten it. On the day before her surgery.

She'd wanted it gone, but not like that.

She had to call up the surgeon when she could talk again. He refused to work on her. That had been worse than then abuse itself. That she might be stuck with a broken unit she didn't even want in the first place.

God, how they'd beaten her. She couldn't remember that part. She didn't want to. She just remembered the pain.

Jess had her network and used it to the fullest. Any possible way to get the emergency surgery that she actually needed. It was a longer-than-long shot, she knew, but she was desperate. These surgeries took months to get in. She'd have to find a surgeon willing to do it that had a cancellation on that very day. Worse than a needle in a haystack. A winning lottery number.

She got replies with numbers. Impossibly, one of them had availability and no one to fill it. No one knew about the surgeon or the practice, but Jess was desperate. Waking up with a vulva was far better than waking up with whatever she was cursed with.

That's what she told herself when she made the call. She repeated it again when she signed on the form, her lower half wrapped with all the ice packs she could find.

The first thing she remembered after the surgery was them apologising. Never something anyone wants to wake up to hear. She tried her best to listen and absorb the information. Extensive nerve damage. Blood vessel damage. Lost blood flow.

In the end, when she finally worked up the nerve to have a peek under the bandage with a mirror, she felt an odd sense of relief. It was definitely a train wreck down there, but it was her train wreck. It was certainly a better train wreck than what the asshole had left her with.

Some things healed. Some didn't.

The room. The building. These she never lost. They left their mark on her, the same way someone could remember all the details when they find out a horrible, world-changing event had occurred. The room was part of her. Part of her memory of clawing to become herself.

She never thought about it consciously. Perhaps in dreams, she'd visited that bed, those walls. She wasn't sure.

Rather than be memories she returned to, they became feelings she carried with her. Part of the woman she would become.

Why did they bring her back here, to where the surgery happened?

The answer was already too clear, as her hoarse throat would no doubt attest.

She'd always thought - assumed - the assault is what made her dissociation so strong. Why wouldn't it have been? The body goes through trauma, the brain detaches itself the best it can, then learns it can do this as a regular thing. Jess learns how to make good use of it. No big deal.

The body is put through trauma, not the body goes through trauma, Jess corrected herself. It's not a passive act.

Not a passive act, Jess thought.

Whatever the hell they did to her was definitely not a passive act. And it wasn't a response to trauma. Dissociation wasn't like this. She knew that, but it was a convenient lie to tell herself because she had no idea what truth she would put in its place. Not until now.

She had never really dissociated. She'd gone within. To the bright expanse that her mind was capable of. To see worlds of possibilities with specific clarity. It wasn't just a good imagination. She had that as a kid. Able to puzzle things out well. Able to solve how to fix the leaky faucet that no one else seemed to get around to.

This was all too different. She'd been enhanced. Tampered with. Given hyper-phantasia and whatever else they managed to slip in. She felt the bitter-sweet pang of an athlete caught doping because the supplements they'd been prescribed contained performance enhancers. She'd been cheating without realising it.

Not that she cared about the rewards, but she had reaped the dividends. She had reaped them when others, no doubt, had not.

Those veils of guilt stayed, but her attention shifted. What had they done to her? It had been too long since she was a daughter of youth. Too much had just become part of her adult life that it felt nearly impossible to tease that apart from who and what she was before surgery.

To her, there would always be a before surgery and an after surgery. After surgery now dominated her mind, her lived experiences, and was a part of countless sexual encounters. Her body, in its current form, she'd already accepted as herself. Everything good and frustrating about it was part of the whole. It was the car she'd grown comfortable with after many years on the road.

Yet, inside this car, inside her, was an interloper. A meddler of the mind. Perhaps also a meddler of the body, though she doubted this. If so, they would have restricted her like they'd done to Roh, she reasoned.

No. Just the mind. The impossible terrain. She'd spent her career mastering its faint vagaries. What she'd been able to design with Beth was heralded as magic. The true bleeding edge.

Or so she thought. Jess realised she knew far less about what was possible.

In her mind, she walked out to the edge of a cliff and looked to the vista that spread ahead of her in all directions. How could she possibly begin to guess the directions they'd explored she didn't know were possible? Even worse, what experiments had they done to learn that knowledge?

To read the brain, to feel as it felt, from the outside was difficult but possible if you were clever. Were they able to not only feel it, but also change it, from the inside? Her mind boggled at the computation power it would take to model the neuron connections of a single person. That was, even if you could get at all of them, which you couldn't. Right? She stopped and stared into the distance in her mind.

Had they – whoever they were – managed to fully map the brain? Not just through fMRI, but something far stronger? She could imagine a government keeping that very secret. How useful it would be for nefarious ends.

Whichever way she tried to solve it, she kept coming to the same conclusion: it simply wasn't possible. She refused to believe they would set aside multiple supercomputers for her. Just one person.

Unless, they really, really needed her for something. She shivered internally at the thought.

That was it, wasn't it? Had they been watching her closely, too? Staying out of her way while she developed? Developed into what, exactly? An autist with persistent fugue states, apparently. She never once did anything that for a moment made her think she was anything special. Sure, skilled and persistent, and she worked hard so she got the inevitable label of "gifted". No supernatural gifts ever showed their face. No levitation. No telekinesis. Nothing that would warrant long-term cloak and dagger attention.

She was going to have to wake up out of this state to gather more data. Nothing she had inside her felt sufficient to answer it on her own.

All she had to do was stir. To break out of this state like she had done thousands of times before. She hadn't solved the problem, but without the data, she wasn't sure she could.

She just needed to wake up. It should be easy.

But she wasn't waking up.

28

THE DOCTOR

"AS YOU CAN SEE, the two women we brought in the other day have been working in the field successfully as originally programmed. We needed only to establish the correct reward system, which as we've known for decades was discovered by my predecessor in the Heartsong project. Here we have two of our test subjects back under observation."

Dr. Pyne spun the tablet he held until it was snuggly under his right arm. "Science Vessel #40981 was given two pushes. First, we allowed her creative states to go deeper and be more prolonged. The second? I must say I'm proud of this one. We nudged her desire for connection a bit higher."

With finality, he swung around to look at his audience. Suits, generals, a mishmash of unsavoury officials. "Longing and skill created a unique opportunity for us. The Bonobo Device is now in 1 out of every 6 households, with projections of being in 1 out of every 4 households by year's end. We will, of course, use the usual surveillance on these devices, which I leave to the soldiers in the field." He gestured absently to one of the generals before turning his attention back to the group as a whole.

"Now, penetration into homes like this we've already done with our work on surveilling the network usage of households. But this. The Bonobo Device." He held the one Jess had taken from Regan's house in his hand for all to see. "This lets us track the thoughts and feelings. A level of transparency never before possible. Soon, we'll be able to do more. Our participant here will continue to work on this device under our supervision. With her work, we'll be able to engage with the public emotionally in ways never before thought possible. The safest populace is a calm populace, as they say."

He took a few steps, to stand such that another patient was in view of the crowd. "Our military vessel is a true specimen. Given only an improved healing factor and deeper spatial and bodily awareness, she managed to develop additional skills. Taken in by this city's underground, she was taught a variety of evasion tactics. In short, without realising it, they trained Military Vessel Rho for penetration and reconnaissance. The vessel already managed both infiltration of one of our facilities and evasion of capture when incapacitated by leveraging interpersonal connections. I'll let Special Agent McGoven brief everyone on the spy potential for similarly augmented vessels."

With this, he fell into a smile that would cause most humans unease to see. "I have been informed that another emergent condition occurred in recent weeks with Science Vessel #40981 and Military Vessel Rho. We have observed they are pair-bonding. While we do allow some pair-bonding between vessels of different types, we have noted that this particular pair-bonding will impede progress on the individual projects and have recommended permanent decoupling."

The doctor cleared his throat. "As we all know, everything is brain structures and brain chemistry. There is no free will. Once we've separated them long enough and rewired their reward systems, they'll have forgotten about each other."

The doctor turned and began walking. "Now onto our next test subjects. Here we can see how effective goal induction therapy combined with military training can be. Myself and Dr. Alabast have been collaborating on a technique we hope you'll find has exceptional results."

29

A NEW LAB

JESS

Jess awoke in the stillness of her new cell. It was a sparse room, with cot and minimal life supporting linens. Her whole body ached, even though she couldn't remember using it. There was something still picking at the back of her mind, scratching away at a door that she never remembered being there before, like a cat wanting to be let out.

How long had she been out?

She'd been exploring the expanse in her mind and then, as minds do, she had faded from that place to this.

She shivered remembering. Not so much exploring as trying to escape. They'd somehow managed to lock her into her own mind, with no key nor lock in sight. It was all too easy to imagine they would do it again and again, for whatever purpose they had in mind.

It'd left her not only dazed, but with a splitting headache to boot.

Jess soaked in her misery as she scanned the room. No obvious exits except for the door she knew would be barred. Towels and clothes that looked fit for a prison. A simple place to sleep that she doubted she'd last more than two nights on before getting back problems.

And them.

Those assholes behind the door, beyond those walls. Whatever they had been doing to her, whatever they had done to her, she felt trapped by it. Lost to it. Whatever fierce machinations they had in progress, whatever role they saw for her, there seemed to be only two choices.

Play the role. Or don't.

To not play the role meant giving up everything. Her life. Her work. Rolling the cosmic dice to see what's on the other side of the unknown.

Leaving Roh. Jess sucked in air. In such a short time, she couldn't imagine giving her up. Something about her made life sweeter. As awful as the last few days had been, close calls and all, that Roh was there. That Jess could reach out and touch her made something solid out of chaos.

Jess dragged her nails along the edge of the cart. She already knew. She didn't even have to ask. They were trying to keep them apart. Force them apart. That door in her mind had something to do with it. She still felt Roh, as if she was against her body, but there was something else there. A kind of cold separation. Like a fight/flight/freeze response was turned on without her permissions and pointed at Roh. There was no reason for her to fear Roh, and yet they'd done something to her so that Roh would appear to be a threat. Worse yet, some of that sweetness had been squelched.

Jess wanted to know how they could do that. Scientific curiosity struck her harder than her own indignation. If she could figure out how, she reasoned, perhaps she could fight back. At the very least, perhaps she could slow them down while she came up with a plan.

Jess formed her initial plan for resistance. They were going to try to pull Roh away, so she wouldn't let them. Simple. At least, in theory. In practice, fighting back was going to require spending every waking moment visualising Roh touching her in places that made her heart open and her body sing. For every bit of rewiring they would do, she would have to do her own. She would have to move where her feeling for Roh lived. Mirror neurons. The cortical homunculus. Anywhere and everywhere. For good measure, she'd also throw in tonglen, an ancient practice of using imagination to wish well to others. It had an important feature she needed: to keep her compassion soft and pliable. While she wanted very much to hate and fight her captors, she knew that it was better to fight them like a river carving through a mountain.

She reached up and pulled her hair behind her ears and sat up straight. She couldn't risk getting caught doing what she was about to do, but she needed to keep her mind and body healthy enough to fight back. Once she'd woken everything up, she should be able to continue doing it surreptitiously.

The meditation retreats. The mind training. Never in a million years did think she'd be using it to fight mind control wars with the government. She wondered idly if she might be able to steal a bit of tin foil during meal times to fashion herself a hat. Maybe it would help.

She let herself smile at her own joke. The wins might be hard to come by, and if she could keep her spirits up, she could keep her energy up as well. That's where she would get the upper hand. As long as she could keep finding herself and doing the work, she could improve her chances. Nothing was a sure thing, but at least she had something to work toward. Having a goal was certainly better for her mental health than not having one.

Jess cursed that she couldn't easily masturbate. That would have made the process a bit easier, though she admitted even if she could, they might easily catch her at it and stop her. If they were trying that hard to pull them apart, it'd be a surefire sign she was fighting back.

Jess trailed a finger along the bare skin of her leg and up to her bunched up prison clothes. Her body was still hers. For now. She closed her eyes and took a breath. That's where she would start. In her own skin. In her own mind.

Just as she got settled and began her practice, her eyes shot open at the sound of a key in the door. Her heart raced. Had they caught her? Had she really so little time to fight back before they would go again?

Two heavies in suits appeared in the room.

"You're up."

———

Jess gaped at the array of technology they'd set out. It easily rivalled her most stocked lab back at work. An intricate array of probes, spectral analysers, biometric machines, and more. In the middle of the room sat a rather terrifying chair she could only assume was meant for whoever was the test subject of the day. She idly wondered if there was enough stuff here to fashion a bomb for their escape.

That was, if she knew where Roh was.

She couldn't risk anything like that without knowing who on was on the other side of the wall. She didn't have to plan long before another spanner was thrown into her mental gears.

"You'll be accompanied by a competent staff members who will aide you in your work for us. They're familiar with the machinery, so you need only ask for what you need. But, let me warn you, they will watch you every step of the way and report back to us. If they think for a second you're working on something that isn't what we asked you to build, we'll know."

The ominous voice was owned by an even more ominous-looking suit. Jess noted she was really starting to get tired of suits. It felt both like corporate hell and a kind of Stepford Wives of devious, diabolical government machinations.

She fought to ignore them. At least the people they'd ushered in to help her had lab coats on. That was a few grains of normalcy in an ocean of chaos. She exchanged pleasantries with them, then set her mind to the task.

The task. She walked over to the table covered in variations on the Bonobo Device. They'd managed to purchase each one. They'd been watching her. Of course they had.

She picked up each and thought about it. The heft of the earlier versions nearly drove them off the market, but they proved too effective to ignore. With time came improvements, and some particularly inspired brainstorming sessions later they had made it to the present day version. Light. Long battery. Well-worth the money for the peace of mind you could buy with it.

Stress, arousal, consent. SAC. That was the foundation of the Bonobo Device since its inception. The goal was accuracy. With that, the other lab paired communication capabilities for alerting authorities. All in a small hardware package that fit snugly in a gem-shaped display. Each version was just improvements on the original idea. Product clarity leading to product success.

The suits did not care about product clarity. Couldn't give a fuck about product impossibility. Just getting basic readings where they wanted the jewel positioned would be impossible, let alone the other features they imagined it would have.

Adding theta wave reading seemed harmless enough, but the device would have to be relocated to the head. They'd ruled out that idea on day one. No one would wear a device on their head. It just wouldn't be fashionable. Not that the suits knew anything about fashion.

She considered just outright refusing, explaining that it was an impossible task where the device was currently situated. She could also explain that moving the device would drop its effectiveness for its primary task until they managed to figure out how to recalibrate it.

Something in her mind told her that pushing back would be absolutely useless. Besides, she had a better idea. A classic of grad schools and industrial labs alike. She was going to stall. Not overtly. She wasn't going to drag her feet. She was actually going to work on what they wanted: additional brainwave detection with the existing Bonobo Devices, perhaps with minor modification. In the original position, not the head. Impossible, she knew, but it didn't matter. She'd worked at impossible tasks before.

The "why" was the important part. Her real goal was one she suspected they wanted next. Not just sensing the SAC states so they could be displayed. She had a different idea, that she suspected was very close to what they had in mind. They would want her to read minds, and so did she. On that point, they agreed.

They'd get their theta wave experiments. Heaps of them. If they wanted data, they'd get it. She might even luck out and solve the very problem they asked. Wouldn't that be funny? Sometimes the impossible becomes solvable because it was never impossible to begin with. People just assumed it was.

She motioned for one of them to grab the EEG headgear they had granted her lab.

"Who's up first? It's time to start getting our baselines."

Baselines that would be very helpful in the days to come.

She grabbed one of the Bonobo Devices, looping it around the neck of the helper. She attached a debug cable to it and set the sensors wide open. If there was any synchronicity between theta waves, she'd find it.

The other data? Oh, don't mind that. That's just collected by the machines. Extra data. Superfluous. She wouldn't bring any attention to it, and she doubted they would either. It would all look exactly as it should.

Hidden in this data was something she was very keen to find. If she couldn't, she'd have to risk taking a broader spectrum reading. She shrugged internally. She'd have to cross that bridge when she got to it.

"Okay, ready?" she asked her first participant.

30

NOBODY'S DEVICE

ROH

Fuck!

Roh's body crashed face-first into the training field, onto a dense foam pad that was only slightly more forgiving than concrete. At that moment, her body felt less forgiving than either of them.

As she pushed herself off the pad, she felt her shoulder socket loosen dangerously. Another fall like this could finish knocking it out, likely tearing it in the process.

"Do it. Again."

The drill instructor asshole was living up to Roh's nickname for him. She looked at the pair of walls set in the room, facing each other less than a metre apart. This fucking asshole wanted her to scale the walls through coordinated jumps. Something that she might be able to pull off fresh on a good day, but this was after an already long day of training.

Timing. It was all in the timing. If that was off, or her grip was off, she'd crash again. These walls were slick and unforgiving. Oppositional forces would have been a better idea, but it still felt like glass.

None of this really made any sense to her.

She'd trained to be a runner. She didn't train to do this. She just needed a task to do. Yet, here they were training her with inefficient motion. If they wanted her to scale something as slick as glass, there were better ways to do it.

Assholes.

At least the assholes Benjar used to train her knew their shit. They were smart. They taught her to learn how her body worked. What it could do. None of this one-size-fits-all nonsense. None of this "I saw this on a training video one time, now you have to do it" nonsense. She was pretty sure the asshole beside her had never done this obstacle as stated before in his life.

That gave Roh an idea.

She lined herself up for more ninja horseshit on the walls. Holding, pinching, turning, kicking in an attempt to gracefully scale both walls by alternating which wall she kicked off it.

This time, maybe as a result of the adrenaline coursing through her at the thought of what she was about to do, she managed to hold tight enough and release quickly enough to make progress. It was still slippery, but she was managing enough friction to move steadily upward.

When she was at least a bit over four metres above the group, instead of going higher, she grabbed the side of the wall and pulled hard, which launched her towards the asshole watching her from below. His body took the full brunt of hers as she crashed into him feet first. His eyes wide that she would attempt something like this.

Roh wasn't sure if she'd killed him, or merely knocked him out, but she set herself to the task of searching him for a key. She needed to get out. She was more than happy to take her chances against who she met in the halls.

Her adrenaline turned to frustration as she found no pockets on the outfit of this drill sergeant. She had just enough time to wonder at his useless clothing before the edges of her vision dimmed.

In a far off place, she heard the sound of clapping. Annoying, rip your ears out clapping. The kind of clapping that only a smug scientist does when he's very pleased with himself.

Roh would have groaned if her body had listened to her. It, however, was already firmly lost to her.

She barely managed to make out the first words out of his mouth. "Bravo. I was guessing it would take you another few sessions to try that. I do so like a good surprise."

With that, her world went dark.

———

Roh's holding cell smelled like piss. She didn't remember entering it. Nor did she remember changing her clothes. She hated the idea that other people, people she didn't give permission to, might have seen her without clothes on.

Her modesty, though, was the least of her concerns. Her body felt pulped. On the plus side, at least it seemed ready to obey her once again. The thought of them being able to usurp control over her body at a moment's notice made her want to retch. She had no clue how to stop them.

That was the root of it. Her body was broken, but her mind was broken too. It ached in a way she'd never felt before. Her inner vault torn from its hinges. Violated. Her volition, once invaluable, now involuntary. A slave to a hidden piper.

Oh how she wanted to tear the walls down and find the fuckwit who thought she could be handled with a remote-control. She was nobody's device.

At that thought, she retched.

She pulled her knees up to her chest and hugged herself. It wasn't enough to hate her new life, whatever was left of it. No, it was more. She felt herself mourning something, too. A different life. Not just her freedom but something special.

Roh gritted her teeth. The only way to fight back was to survive. Giving up was not an option worth considering. Revenge. Now that would be delicious if she could be patient enough, and quick enough, to manage it. What happened after would be well worth it.

They'd never let her leave. She knew that.

At least she could go out in style. No fading away. Only fury.

31

CALM FOCUS AND NAUGHTY TRICKS

JESS

Jess sat on the edge of her cot, her body heavy with the work of the day, wrung out by the toll the week had taken. Keeping her mind clear enough to make mental notes while not getting caught had been a torturous challenge. Keeping her face neutral as they worked turned her stomach.

The only thing keeping her afloat was her nightly practice. She balled up the pillows, which let her sit up in bed without looking like she was doing more than resting. Then, she went inside. A tumult of fatigue, mixed images, fuzzy projections of the future stirred around in her mind at night, but she knew them to all be illusions. Like how the surface scattering of light wasn't able to hold a true reflection of the sun. It was only once the pond stilled could the sights be taken in.

Jess had to admit, in recent years she'd let her practise lapse. It was hard to hold on to it with the demands of work and the push-pull of her social life. Difficult too because so much of it felt other-worldly. She couldn't force herself to believe in any kind of afterlife, let alone reincarnation. It was populated by too much of what seemed to curse humankind: wishful thinking.

Perhaps those fundamentals were solid after all. Mind training was absolutely what she needed. For thousands of years, that's exactly what people had been studying and practising. The mind, and the brain as its home, were facile. Not formless, certainly, but changeable. With enough practice, one could cause enough change that the rudimentary devices to observe the brain could see the difference.

She didn't know if they'd be able to sense what she was doing, but if she was honest, she didn't care. Instinctively, she knew to best pull off what she was attempting in the lab was to go into that lab bright and caring, not showing the least bit of aggression that would cause them to resist. Obviously, being overtly caring and kind would also raise red flags. It had to instead be internal and as genuine as she could be. To literally soften her own heart as a way of bringing ease to others. After all, what she planned wouldn't hurt them. There was no reason for them to feel threatened.

The best deception is not to deceive.

Jess sat staring at the wall, and an idea formed in her head. It would be a monumental feat. She wasn't even sure it was possible. Still, the kernel of an idea formed.

And it would definitely require some amount of deception.

She thought back to reading papers with Beth. It would be possible to go much further than they were asking her, but she would need some help. She would need access to their own research. Combined with what she already knew, she just might be able to pull it off.

She slowly breathed out.

She let that idea sit in her mind. Helping them do what they're doing might be the worst plan. Jess could only guess at how much damage they would cause with access to everyone's Bonobo. Especially once she made whatever modifications they ultimately requested. She resolved to not let it get that far. She had to succeed.

One in and out breath to steady herself, then she focused.

Her thoughts turned from her own stories towards wishing well on each person she had encountered. On the building as a whole. On the city they were in. Transmuting, in her mind, the confusion and frustrations that would lead people to hurt others into something more useful.

She knew the practice was unlikely to actually change them, which she thought far too fanciful. The science was there, though, that showed it would change her. That was exactly what she wanted. A salubrious mind, one softened and less likely to knee-jerk, was more useful to her. For what she was planning, she was going to need all that and more.

She was feeling worse, and each day would get harder.

Slowly, softly, she corrected herself. The future didn't even exist — yet. She should pace herself, but worrying too much about what she had no control over wouldn't do. Worry led to poor sleep. Poor sleep meant poor recovery. Shitty mattress meant shitty back support. It wasn't rocket science.

On the in-breath, she inhaled greed and suffering. On the out-breath, she gave back generosity and clarity.

As she steadied herself, her thoughts shifted to Roh. She didn't even know if she was still alive. A fucking terrifying thought. Of course they would keep them apart, and it was annoyingly effective at making her imagine the worst.

She sent out a positive thoughts to Roh. One she doubted would reach her lover, but who knew? Maybe it was possible when people were connected to each other. She doubted it, but what the hell.

Feeling the tension in her body as she tried to relax, she had to admit it. At this rate, she likely could only keep going for a week. Seven days, and likely little more, before they really managed to break her down.

One week. All her hopes rested on the days ahead.

———

"Absolutely not," the voice sounded disembodied in its recoil. It was owned by the laboratory sector head, a wiry man who looked sown to his lab coat. His office was of modest decoration, but she couldn't help but spot a part of the wall with an inordinate amount of tiny plaques. She was sure the plaques meant something, but surely nothing to anyone outside of their fevered inner circle.

He hadn't moved a muscle since his dismissal of her idea. He just stared at her, like they were about to play chess for their lives and he had been training for this very moment.

"Dr. Falcone, if I could look through the research, I would have a much easier time than knowing what I don't know. Of closing the gaps. I can increase the sensitivity, but if you have correlation data that I don't have, my task becomes doable on a much shorter timeline."

He shook his head and then waited, staring at her. "All you need are readings data for our near-field research?"

"That's all. I suspect you found things I never did. The combination would be incredibly helpful."

Dr. Falcone sighed. "I think you're wasting your time, but I doubt you'll be able to do much damage with them. We'll release them to you. But you have to remember something. With this comes expectation. With this, we'll be watching you even closer. Without good results, a line of experimentation gets cut."

He stood and looked at her. "Now, are we done? Is there

anything else?" he asked, but his voice betrayed no sense of benevolence.

"There is one other thing," Jess said, her voice now barely above a whisper.

———

She hadn't expected them to say yes, but here she sat on a couch in the lab.

It wasn't subtle. Push or die. Like the hell weeks to write her academic research, only this time for her life. She drummed her fingers on the roller table she's pushed up to the sofa as a kind of bedside table, and then stared at the cameras they'd installed.

She opened the documents they'd given her and read through them. Unsurprisingly, they contained plenty she had never known was possible. Jealous, to be sure, but her curiosity grew.

It all gave her a terrible idea.

On a whim, she started checking for weak points like Benjy's team had taught her. Any possible point of code ingress. They had to be there. For all their advanced biotech, something told her that their security was probably a bit lax by comparison.

She did her best not to look up at the cameras to see if they could make out what she was doing. Hell, she worried about tensing a little too much.

It took hours. Lab techs came and went, asking her questions about the research and what was next.

Finally, she managed to find one possible way in using a trick they taught her. Jess mentally crossed her fingers they wouldn't burst through the door, and then she pulled up her software terminal and got to work.

32

NOT ONE WASTED MINUTE

ROH

Roh was feral. Livid.

"Look, I'm tired of this bullshit," she spat. "Whatever games you're playing, that's it. I'm done. This training course is worthless, you're literally trying to train me to be worse. What's the fucking point?"

The trainer just looked at her.

"Oh, is that how this is going to play out. You're going to do what you're told and I'm just going to let you because you're really just a pawn, too? Well, then go get the fucker in charge so we can have a real conversation about this. Look, I'm willing to sit and talk. Hell, I'm willing to do jobs. But whatever this is? Less than worthless. I'm not even getting good exercise."

She changed tack. "Look, I'm not a violent woman. I'm not here to start a war. If I knew what you wanted, I'd have a better chance of helping you. Keeping me in the dark is just going to make this all take longer."

She gave it one last try. "I know I'm stuck here. You already own me. I get it. Just let me work with you."

Then she shut her mouth and stared, giving her best 'come on, man!' expression.

He said nothing and instead pointed at the pegboard now installed into the room.

Roh walked over and grabbed two of the pegs from the box. "I don't need that much upper body strength. If I get more, it'll move my centre of gravity. I'll go backward." Then, resolved to her fate, she began working the board.

After an hour of it, she put her hands in the air. "No, I'm done. I want to talk to someone."

Instead of staring at her, the soldier got up and left the room. Roh figured it was either going to turn out poorly, or worse, but her arms burned with unnecessary pain, which had become a constant of her imprisonment.

She leaned her back against the pegboard and waited.

Roh did not expect what happened next. Less than a minute after leaning against the board, the door flew open and a guy larger than any she'd ever seen ran at her full speed. She didn't have time to think. She jumped up hard and pushed with all her might as the brute came at her, flowing with her body as she somersaulted over him. As she flipped, she caught him by the neck with her interlocked hands and completed her rotation by digging her heels in the back of his knees.

It worked. The brute dropped hard, crashing into the board with the remainder of his momentum.

Roh jumped off him, her jaw slack, her pulse racing. What the fuck. No one had ever taught her how to pull off a move like that. That it worked shocked her.

That she knew how to do it in the first place terrified her. What had they been doing to her when she wasn't conscious?

The sound of the door opening only vaguely registered in her awareness. Followed by the distant sound of footsteps and an all-too-familiar voice going "tsk tsk".

Roh didn't raise her head. She'd already been beaten.

"Why so sad, my little robot of flesh? Have you finally

realised that not a moment of your training was wasted? We took such care with you, why would we be frivolous now? Such doubt is unbecoming. We know exactly how we want you to be made. I think the results speak for themselves, don't you?"

Roh couldn't even groan as her vision faded.

———

Roh's cell didn't feel as constricting as the cell in her mind. She barely felt like herself anymore. Her thoughts were there, but simmering in all directions was the terror of knowing she was no longer her own. At any moment, the thought she could be tossed into action as if she were on remote control lingered in her mind. And like remote controls, there was no wire she could find to cut off their access.

She just had to take it.

She fucking hated having to take it.

The opportunities she wished would materialise around revenge didn't seem to. The moment one of the scientists was in view, her vision was already blurring, and her muscles stopped responding to her commands.

Then they'd throw her in here when they were done with whatever experiments they'd done to her. An emptiness worse than indoctrination. More like a toy. A machine.

What did he call her?

A 'robot of flesh'. Fuck. No. Ew.

Roh thought about a mouse in a maze she saw as a child. She always wondered if the mouse felt anything. Fear about being stuck in the maze. Glory at finding the cheese. Misery at being in a lab, in some experiment. None of them were really the life of a mouse. What was the life of the mouse? Whatever the mouse chose. But a caged mouse was safer than a mouse in the wall stealing food at night, her guardian had said. She thought about that. What was safety when her hours and days were taken from her? Isn't that which steals your life slowly as bad as that which threatens to take it quickly?

She dug her stubby nails she refused to chew into the frame of the bed and pulled hard, tearing at whatever coating they'd put on it. It did little to soothe her nerves.

She stared at the door and dared it to open.

33

TO GIVE AND TO RECEIVE

JESS

Jess hadn't slept in 30 hours. She'd read more papers than she'd thought possible. In her search, she also managed to find to hit the jackpot. There was enough incriminating evidence on their experiments to blow a hole in their works. The trouble was smuggling it out. So that's what she put her mind to.

By the end, her eyelids were violent sandpaper over blood-shot eyes. She didn't dare wonder how she managed to put lines of code together, let alone lines of thought. She just did it, like the machine she was building. This was going to be her master-piece. And, like a magnum opus, she might only have one.

Operating this thing with sufficient sleep would be a herculean task. Operating it without sleep? More than ill-advised. It might be enough to drive her mind past the brink. To splinter it in the voices of those around her.

She stood back and looked at it, shocked that no one in the lab had tried to stop her. After a point, her brain slipped into autopilot, yet she still managed to keep them at bay.

This thing, a complete mess of wires and a formidable looking strap that would run around her head, and a pair of gloves carefully lined with sensors and transmitters that would connect up to the rest of the device. Like some horror machine, yet she was about to put it on.

It was a – if she dared allowed herself the compliment – *sophisticated* piece of machinery. It's primary task was one of sending and receiving, to send out her own feelings and receive someone else's. Amplified a bit, based on the research she could find, but only a bit. The secondary capability is where the strength really came on. The gloves, having been attached to her sensors, were able to transmit her feelings in an even stronger way. The disadvantage, of course, was she had to actually touch the person she wanted to transmit to.

Feelings at a distance. Stronger feelings at a touch. Though, she hadn't dared test the device on anyone in the lab. The second they felt her, they would have found out.

The best science is untested, isn't it? Didn't someone say that?

She'd studied mindfulness, and how thoughts cascade in the mind. The way a thought, or a worry, bounces around inside of us. A doubt becomes a fear becomes a jealousy becomes a violence. All her work tried to make violence less likely, in all of its forms. If she wasn't careful with this new device, though, she'd cause harm. After all, it was her mind that was about to have to do the biggest lift it ever had.

She wished more than once she'd spent a few years in a cave to be ready for this moment. Wishing didn't make it so, as they said.

"Enough," Jess whispered to herself, firming her resolve. "Let's do this."

———

The door swung open on two unsuspecting lab workers and a guard behind them. Their eyes went wide as they took in

Jess, who was now covered in a wire harness and a large backpack.

"What the fu..." one of them started before dropping to their feet as Jess gently reached out and touched them. The look of concern on their face melted into one of tranquillity. The guard behind them reached for a gun, so Jess took a breath, feeling his anger and fear. In its place, as she exhaled, she fought to send a sense that there was no reason to fight her. She had no reason to do anyone any harm. Nor did he need to harm her to protect himself or anyone here.

He hesitated.

Jess tried to push slightly harder. To offer him rest. To offer him a chance for an easier path than that of the gun. At that, his shoulders slouched.

"That's right, rest," she said, slowly walking up to him. When she was close enough, she reached out and touched him lightly at the elbow, then guided him down to sit against the wall.

"Where is the experiment named Roh?" she asked him, locking her eyes with his somewhat-glazed expression.

He answered as if sitting in a field of flowers. "Vessel Rho is two floors down from here. Room 605. Maybe 607."

Close enough. Jess leaned in. "Thank you, that's very helpful of you."

Jess tried her best to navigate the halls without being seen, but lacking peripheral vision because of a large mesh cage over her head definitely did not help.

Her lack of clear vision wasn't her main problem, though. If she didn't have her thoughts right, as she experienced all too well with the next two people who saw her, her nudges could drive them into more aggression, not less.

As the anger crossed over their faces, she lunged forward, hoping the touch would save her. And it did. So far. If either had failed, she would have been an easy target for the emotional recoil she had caused.

It was the next person who showed her the error in her plans.

Thick and iron-clad, this fed was built more like a brick shithouse than the other guards. A statesman of no-fucks-given. As Jess drew this man's feelings into her, her stomach wretched. A cold, dark place swirled inside and boiled over, scorching every surface in her mind. He knew who he was, he had no doubts. His world didn't include any space for her. More than just apathy, she was a merely an inconvenience, and she felt it.

Jess braced herself. As he slowly stepped towards her, she tried her best to push a positive thought towards him. Instead, his feelings hammered at her mind as she did her best to send something to replace his thoughts.

Extra. Redundant. Unnecessary. Each word rammed its way around her mind. She tried pushing again. Nothing.

Expendable. Contaminant. Dead weight. It was his thoughts now that dominated her mind, connecting to all the doubt that stood ready, like a row of neuroreceptors set for loathing. Maybe she wasn't doing the world any favours with her work. Maybe she should shrink into a dot and never take up anyone else's space. Who did she think she was, going off on her own, trying to save the world with her high ideas and higher ideals? What did she know about how the world really worked?

She stared at him as he approached. She was just like him, the tendrils that wrapped around her mind told her. Just like him. She saw so many things as expendable. The animals she ate. The clothes she wore and who made them. The endless streams of devices she bought, each made with hands she would never meet the owners of. Everything she owned. Everything she consumed. Not even an afterthought. Just more lubricant for the gears. She wanted to care for them. She wanted to reach out. But she didn't know their faces. Their names. Their stories. She could wish them well all she wanted, but it was impersonal. A surface wish, if that. What was the difference between outright not caring and giving lip service? Was there any difference to the recipient? She was the same.

As she inhaled again, she took both of them in. She didn't resist the darkness anymore, for she knew she held it in herself as well. She inhaled the darkness they both possessed, those thoughts of sculpting a world to suit yourself, or letting it be sculpted for you without protest. The sameness of their egocentrism. The hearts that were welded shut by opportunity, seared so that its tender wound was no longer open to the actual pains of the world.

She screamed.

She hadn't intended to. For all she could, she wanted to keep silent to improve her chances. But she felt it. Those stitches in her own heart that kept her tucked and numb. With all the willpower she could muster, she ripped at them, a surgery of thought and emotion to her deepest part.

Jess felt them in there with her. The bumps and bruises, by the thousands, that had hardened parts of her. The experiments these assholes had done to her, the parts of her they'd left open to make her want more. Every callus. Every knot in her stomach that kept her safe in the dark. Every sharp word she used to keep a meeting under her control.

It was then she saw it. The look on his face. Not at the scream. He was feeling something, too. She couldn't tell what, but writ large across his face was a change. A kind of cracking of something within.

She reached up. He'd stopped just short of her, close enough that she could gently grab his elbow. Just as it had before, that touch soothed its recipient.

"I need you to take me downstairs. We're going to find Vessel Rho."

He nodded.

"Freeze!" Not even a second after he'd nodded, Jess swung around to a group of guards. She knew she shouldn't have screamed.

This time, she didn't hesitate. She quickly inhaled and pushed into them what she now realised she must have pushed into the heavy who was about to take her downstairs: the sense of broken longing we all carry around because the world is what it is. The truth of our own needs going unmet because of things outside of our control. The wish we all had to find actual connections, whether or not we dared to admit it.

Tears poured down the guards' faces. They looked at her, and she nodded to them gently, offering up her hands. After being sure to touch each of them, she turned again to her guide. "We should go before more show up."

34

AT YOUR COMMAND

ROH

Someone was at the door.

Roh coiled like a snake ready to strike. The first person to open her door was going to feel the fullness of what they'd been training her to do. She figured she could take out at least one person before they took over her mind. What happened after that? Future be damned. It was time for vengeance.

They wanted to teach her to hurt. To destroy. That's exactly what they were going to get. As many as she could get her hands on, she would fight until they dropped her.

The person at the door was fussing with the lock. Why hadn't they got it opened yet? The oddity of it made her pause. Only just. She was still going to tear their fucking throat out. Goddamn, she was tired of this place.

The door finally swung open to show a large fed, solid and muscular, and a shorter science type covered in wires and gizmos. She didn't recognise either of them. Probably here to drag her to more experiments. She pounced.

The big guy was her first target. He looked like he could handle himself in a fight, or at least could ten years ago. Still probably a challenge. She doubted the scientist was much of a fighter, but that thing she was wearing spooked her. Definitely was not going to let her get close.

The force of her body crashing into the man above his centre of gravity caused him to spill backward, first against the door frame, and then out into the hall.

"Roh, wait!" the scientist yelled at her. Funny, Roh thought. Why would she know her name? Roh guessed all the scientists probably knew most of the active experiments. Probably easier to control people with that hint of familiarity. Roh thought about all this in the split second it took to turn and land on her feet and sprint down the hall.

She could hear the scientist take off after her. As if this woman had any hope of catching her.

"Roh, stop! Why are you running?"

Why do you think? To get away from sketchy looking scientists, Roh thought. Something tugged at her mind, then. It felt like nostalgia, or that feeling of smelling the pillow a lover used after they left. A kind of longing that had an explanation.

She stopped in her tracks and spun on the lady following her. Perhaps the woman could be her out. While jumping out of the window had worked once, she had no idea how many floors up they were.

While a voice in her head told her to keep her distance from this persistent woman covered in tech, she needed a hostage. She still might have to jump out a window, but she needed to slow them down first.

She didn't have time to do either. Before she could move, the edges of her vision clouded, and her body stopped responding. Somewhere, in the back of her mind, a loud command sounded.

KILL HER

35

POWER OF A HUG

JESS

Jess' heart dropped. To see someone who already had so much of her heart look at her if she didn't recognise her at all was too much. It was so much worse to watch those same eyes change from unfeeling to murderous.

She'd seen this look before in ex-lovers. Right before they'd sent her scrambling to find a hospital. The thought, the memory, froze her in place. Gone was any thought of trying to reach out to this person. Gone, too, was the space to feel anything for her.

She'd already lived this. Searching a lover's face in confusion and disbelief they'd turn on her. Hoping they remembered anything of the care she once believed they had, only for it all to be replaced with anger. She promised herself she'd never let it happen again, and here they were.

Gone, too, was any thought of using the device to calm her down. She wanted to incapacitate this person.

That's what it felt like to Jess. This person. This other human being. Not a lover anymore. Not three-dimensional. But a flat, two-dimension threat to her person. She didn't care what made them tick. She just wanted them gone and out of her life.

Somewhere in the back of her mind, etched on screen near a blinking cursor, were the risk factors she had previously identified. The cursor sat next to one that said, "they want to tear us apart". Unfortunately, her cold, logical self had been covered in the stink and the sheen of fear, buried as a distraction, and shoved far, far into the back of her mind.

Roh rocked a bit on the balls of her feet, taking a predator's posture as she watched Jess.

Jess wasn't sure she wouldn't even survive her first attack, looking at her now. Roh's hands readied for a grapple. Her whole body tensed like a spring.

The fear shifted. From staring at an abuser before they hurt her to one of staring down the barrel of a gun she had no control over. A sense of "it can't be helped". Her life would be snuffed out by this woman she thought she knew. Jess realised, she couldn't understand anyone who would take a life. Here she was about to lose hers, and she understood even less. She'd done nothing to provoke this woman, but it didn't matter. It didn't before, and it didn't now.

Jess barely registered the sound of clapping echoing in the halls, Her eyes stayed fixed on the panther of a woman in front of her ready to strike.

"I see you two found each other again. How fitting. I couldn't think of a better way to end a disobedient experiment than by having an obedient one tear her apart." His voice sounded familiar, but Jess couldn't place it.

Out of the corner of her eye, Jess caught someone walking along the walk to stand near them. She chanced a quick glance before locking her eyes back on Roh. A scientist, complete with an obnoxiously pretentious lab coat worn outside the lab. She'd seen him before. He was there after her surgery, a shadow on another man who jotted things down on a tablet. Rarely spoke back then, but time had apparently cured him of any shyness.

"You'll have to forgive vessel Rho. She's not really here right now. She's a bit more animal than human, and once I give the command, you'll see she's also quite the capable fighter. I'm more than a little proud of this one, I have to say. You should have seen what she managed to do to some of the trainers we sicced her on."

This guy would not shut up.

"Just get it over with," Jess spat her own words back at him. She readied herself.

"Bossy, bossy. Someone is used to being in charge. Trust me, I'll unleash her when I choose, and only when I choose. And you'll get to see what a successful experiment really looks like. Look at you. You look a mess. How were we supposed to use all that?"

The asshole gestured at Jess, and she looked down briefly. Her devices! She was covered in them. They did something that could help her, but she fought to remember how.

"Still, you managed to escape, I'll give you that. Not a complete failure. Just, well, any rat that escapes its cage can't be trusted. I'm sure you understand. You were clever enough to flee the cage, but we weren't testing you for lock-picking. Besides, we can't have test subjects wandering around in the halls like this. It just won't do."

At least when Roh killed her, she wouldn't have to hear this guy's unending stream of vocalised flatulence.

It did, however, give her an idea.

"Come on already." She spread her own hands at her side, her arms taut. "You're going to put me to sleep."

"Oh, you'll do more than sleep," he retorted lazily. "Well, since you seem so insistent. It'll be over soon, I assure you."

The moment he looked down to type into a tablet, Jess sprang. She wrapped her arms around him and pulled with all her might to move him between her and Roh.

To her surprise, his body relaxed. Like the clang of a hammer clanging against a bare anvil, a thought hit her. That thought stretched time long enough she could hear herself think. The devices. The wires. The pads on her hands. They all had a point. She was trying to remind others how to feel.

Finally, she concentrated and sent a single thought into the guy in her arms. *We are human, flesh and blood. We are not rats.*

He didn't say anything, but Jess' instincts told her that wasn't enough. She chanced one more thought, condensed and stilled her breath as she thought it.

You are interconnected with us.

His body shuddered. His arm moved as he typed something into the tablet, only to drop it on the ground. Jess dared to look up. She needed to know if she'd at least stopped the beast. Both of them.

Instead, her mouth dropped. Roh's eyes filled, tears streamed down her face. Jess gaped. How could someone one minute stare murder at her, and the next such softness?

A tablet laid on the floor beneath them. Despite all her instincts telling her to keep watching the threat in front of her, her eyes dropped to the device now face up on the floor. Its screen read "Factory Reset: Successful." A sick joke?

Jess jumped as she felt Roh's arms wrap around her, the scientist all but forgotten as he slid to the floor.

"You did it, babe. You did it!"

Jess could hear the words. She knew at some level what they meant. But processing of speech lagged behind the rush of adrenaline that flooded every part it could reach. She was still in danger. She was still going to get murdered. They weren't safe. Roh was going to turn on her. The scientist was going to turn them in. Someone was going to see them in the hall.

They were going to die.

And still, Roh hung on.

36

A SMALL KINDNESS

ROH

"Buttercup, we need to go."

She could tell she felt different now. The shadows that always lingered in the corners of her mind were gone. Whatever Jess had done to Dr. Pyne had him crumpled to the floor. And, more importantly, he had set her free.

Judging from Jess' face, things weren't going so well moments before, but try as Roh did, she couldn't remember anything. How long had they been in the facility? She only remembered entering the door. Everything after that was cloudy, but something told her time had passed. A lot of time. Her body felt heavier, stronger.

The woman in her arms shook, so she relaxed and looked at her. Jess' brow furrowed, her eyes pools of worry. Something definitely had gone horribly wrong.

"We need to get out of here," she said as firmly and calmly as she could. "And our friend here is going to help us." Roh loosened her grip on Jess, then bent down and picked up the mini tablet on the floor and the keycard at the scientist's hip. He was out cold. She looked back at Jess, who still had all the features of a rabbit under a hawk. "Can you trust me enough to follow me, so I can get us out of here?"

Jess didn't even nod, so Roh took her by the wrist. Thankfully, her body seemed to not resist her.

Roh didn't know why, but she quickly found out she knew the building like the back of her hand. She'd been here before, when she was younger, but they never let her roam much. And yet, every turn, every room, every elevator was at ready access in her mind.

She led them to a service elevator and hit the button. The stir of the elevator was ungodly slow, probably meant for supplies and little else. All Roh could feel as she waited was gratitude and the residual stench of fear.

One service elevator led to a hallway past a galley, then to another service elevator. The people here who noticed them kept quiet and ignored them, and Roh thanked each with a nod. One of the workers walked up to them and reached out a hand.

Roh bit her lip gently as she took the security pass. A small gesture, but they had to have seen so much here. She mouthed her thanks as they headed down to the basement via the emergency escape.

Roh nodded at the worker as the elevator door shut. Another little kindness passed between them as she reached over and gently grabbed Jess' hand. She felt her flinch, and then a minute relaxing.

Little victories, Roh thought. That's how the world gets rebuilt. Little victories.

37

NEWSFLASH

JESS

Regan stared at them with a look of a vampire catching sight of a fresh wound.

"We're going to tell everyone. I want to tear holes in them. I want to see them bleed."

Jess wasn't far off with her vampire assessment. "I'm beat, Reg. If I never hear about them, or see anything about them, ever again..."

"You won't have to, I'll handle it." Regan picked up the tablet. "But they aren't getting away with this." She looked down at the tablet in disbelief. "How did they think they were ever going to get away with any of it? No. Not on my watch. Not for what they did to you."

On the table laid a portable drive, a rather hacked medical device, and a tablet. Two of the three could bring the organisation down, if put in the right hands.

"Tell me again what you have."

The numbness poured through Jess, as Beth held her from one side and Roh from the other. She could only sit and listen.

"She's got it all," Beth explained. "There are hundreds of

records on that drive. They span... decades. It's unfathomable how much they got away with, all under our noses."

Regan gently picked up the tablet. "And this?"

"That was the other piece of the puzzle. That's Dr. Pyne's tablet. With that, we were able to interpret the records, including Roh's. The amount of genetic experimentation across all those cases... those people... is obscene."

Regan set the device back down and pulled out her own. "Can we summarise this into something the news agencies can use?"

Beth replied, "Sure, I can help with that. As much as I'd like her help, I think it's best if we leave Jess out of it."

"Fucking hell, way out of it," Roh agreed.

The lawyer surveyed her scene. "I'll do my best, but she'll no doubt need to get questioned."

"On one condition," Roh stated, her voice short and direct.

Regan turned to her. "What's that?"

"That this never happens again. To anyone."

"HEY," Jess said as she crossed across the room and sat on the couch.

Roh set her tablet to the side. "Hey."

"Didn't mean to disturb your game." Jess mumbled in nearly a whisper.

Roh shook her head. "Don't worry about it. I can race later. What's going on?" She turned to face Jess, pulling her feet up onto the couch.

The attention, and the pause from Jess, held the air taut.

"Hey," Roh said again, careful not to make any accidental contact.

It was then that Jess turned to her, this woman who lived with her. Who tried to keep things going after the most harrowing experience of her life. The woman who – for a brief moment – wanted to kill her.

The months that followed their escape had not been easy. Yet, neither of them gave any indication of wanting to give up. Most days were just going through the motions. Being careful of the space. Everyone making sure not to make any sudden movements.

It would wear on anyone, but Roh showed no signs of fatigue.

"What do you want for dinner?" Jess asked as her attention returned. Roh was looking at her, staring in that knowing way she had.

"What is it?" Roh asked.

Jess opened her mouth and then closed it. At last, she signed. "I had something I wanted to bring up, but I thought maybe it would be better to talk about it over dinner."

Food meant comfort, and at least for the last couple of months, food had meant something they could do together that felt safe. It wasn't touching. And it certainly wasn't anything more intimate. Yet, the care they put into everything from making sauces to chopping vegetables felt like something.

Jess held out her hands. Roh paused, and slowly, gently laid her hands inside of Jess'.

"It sounds like you want to talk about it now," Roh suggested. In return, she got a firm nod.

"I've been working on something downstairs that I wanted to show you." At that, she gave another sigh. "A bit too much, if I'm honest. I haven't been this excited about a project in years. It might even get me out of retirement."

The weight of trying to recover from being held captive. The burden of pushing herself beyond any point she ever had before. Of all the pieces she wished she could forget. The images that forced themselves into her dreams over and over. There was no way for her to keep working, not like she had been. Jess tried to quit, but the company insisted on an extended leave of absence. She ultimately agreed, with little hope she'd return.

For weeks, she didn't want to touch any technology, and definitely had no desire to spend time in her lab. It was tough going. Roh tried her best to help, to be supportive, but she quickly learned that her presence just made stressful situations more stressful, and gave her space.

Eventually, Jess would disappear into her lab and reappear, uninterested in talking about what she had worked on. For the most part, Roh assumed she was just blowing off steam, like all the girls who would spend hours under the hood of a car.

Yet here she was, seemingly ready to talk.

"Do you want to tell me about it?" Roh asked.

Jess leaned forward a little. "Before I tell you about it, I want you to promise me something. The minute... No, the second you feel uncomfortable, you say so, and we stop."

Roh instinctively raised her eyebrow but didn't say anything at first. Then, she replied, "Okay, I can agree to that, but I still would like to know what we're talking about."

"I made something."

They both let those three words hang in the air. That Jess had made something new. She was excited about it, even. It all felt a bit too fragile.

"Do you want to show me?" Roh asked, relaxing her fingers into Jess'.

"I'll get them, just sit there. And remember the promise."

Roh pursed her lips. "I remember. I do. I'll wait here."

Jess bolted up and jogged down the stairs as Roh watched. Her enthusiasm shifted the air from tense and tenuous to electric. Something about this made Roh nervous, something she rarely admitted to herself ever feeling.

A minute passed. Then another. As the third minute began, Roh heard the pitter-patter of feet on the stairs.

Excitedly, Jess put two devices in front of them. They looked like Bonobo Devices, but larger, with thick bands. To Roh, they looked a bit like the device she had worn to dampen her tracking signal, yet something about these made them feel quite a bit more alien.

"A Bonobo Device?" Roh wondered aloud. "I didn't think they'd work on me."

At that, Jess beamed an enormous smile. Her face held light like a child's. "I fixed yours so it will work for you."

Roh gave a solid 'huh' and looked on.

"These are my prototypes. They need a bit of work, but should serve as a demonstration."

Roh chuckled. "Now I know how being in one of your meetings feels like."

Jess' smile remained plastered to her face. "These, though," she said, touching them affectionately. "These do something special." She looked into Roh's eyes. "They make you feel."

Roh's mouth hung open, not quite sure what to believe from what she was hearing.

"Which is why it's important to have consent with this thing. A lot of consent. When we wear these, I will feel how you are feeling, and you will feel me."

Roh shook her head. "How is that even possible?" She gently lifted up the device in front of her. "How can these things do that?"

Jess lifted her own device in her hands. "Through the edge of science that's public and a fair amount that isn't. I made sure that all it does is a sense, a feeling. Nothing invasive. Nothing that's meant to hurt."

Realising she'd been looking down at the device, Roh turned to see Jess staring at her.

"You okay?" Jess asked. "I'm sorry, I should have warned you a bit better. I wasn't thinking."

Roh lightly set her device back down. "Yeah, I'm okay. I trust you. I've never once watched you do something to try to hurt someone. I just need a minute."

"Sure, no worries, babe." It was out of Jess' mouth before she realised what she'd said. She hadn't used a pet name in a long while. They felt closer than she felt. They felt like sex and sweat, too, neither of which they'd done since before their capture. Jess watched the other woman, and as their eyes locked, a wave of sadness worked through her. Roh, never one to be vulnerable, suddenly felt desperately raw.

Steadying herself, Jess pressed on. "We have so much to say, I think. So much we're afraid to say. I was hoping that these new Bonobos might help us say them. And feel them. To get us over these – I don't know – barriers. Thorns. Whatever we want to call them. I can't feel you from outside, and it's hard for me to let you in. But if with this I can feel you every step of the way, maybe that'll help us take a step forward."

She took a big breath after that, as if she's just broken the surface in a long swim.

Again, she reached out and held Roh's hand. "We don't have to try it."

"I want to." Roh's voice held firm, though the words came out like sandpaper. To punctuate her words, she gave a sharp affirmative nod. "Let's do this."

Jess, now cooled from her previous glow, lifted her Bonobo Device up and slipped it around her neck. "You just put it on like the early devices. Then, give it a minute. It'll sync up to you, and then it'll vibrate to let you know it's ready."

"After that?" Roh asked, pulling her own device up off the couch.

"After that, there's a button on the front. We'll press and hold at the count of three, then let go at the same count. It's a little clunky, but I'm sure Beth will be able to fix that."

Roh wrapped the device around her neck and then motioned with her fingers. "So we press and hold for three?"

"You got it."

Jess gave them two even counts after their devices were ready, and they followed her instructions. Then, they waited.

"How do we know when it's working?" Roh asked.

Jess smiled at her with all the confidence of being the best in her field. "You'll know. Just give it a few more seconds."

Jess, in all her calm, still found herself wordless when the device kicked in. It was if her inner world now had multiple players. Her thoughts and feelings stayed there, at the head of the table. But now the table was no longer empty, save for her. Now, sitting across from her, was another person. Fully formed and nearly tangible. She felt her thoughts reach out to this new entity, sniffing at it like a dog would.

"Roh?"

Roh's eyes were wide, the head trip well-and-truly in effect. "Is that you?" she asked, her voice distant.

"Yes, that's me, babe," Jess replied. "Just try to relax for a second and let your brain get used to it."

"How's that possible?" Roh's voice didn't sound afraid, in the way that watching someone levitate would be more curiosity-inducing than fear-inducing.

In response, Jess stroked the back of Roh's hand.

"I can feel you. While you were speaking. I could feel how..."

It was then, Jess realised she was watching a tear roll down Roh's face. Soon her own tears flowed freely.

"Yes, it's me. It's me," Jess repeated as she held Roh's hands, crying together as they felt each other.

"God, you're beautiful." Roh broke, no longer able to hold back the emotion. A steady stream from both eyes drew lines down her face. "So beautiful."

At that, Jess couldn't hold back. She launched herself into Roh's arms, pulling her tight. In reply, she felt Roh's muscular arms squeeze her back, strong enough to feel like a vice teasing her ribs.

Love, pure and clear, flowed between them. Like coming upon a spring after a long hike, they drank deeply from it.

It was Jess who moved first. Releasing Roh, she leaned back a bit and cupped Roh's face. "Roh," she began, the emotions swirling heavily as the sense of Roh grew in her mind. "Roh, I want to kiss you."

"Please." A simple request, yet punctuated by the tears that refused to stop.

Jess drew their lips together. Just a kiss. Yet, as they touched, fireflies of feeling danced in Jess' mind. Like fairies holding hands to celebrate an endless spring, her emotion flowed from Roh's body and from Roh's heart. The effect intoxicated her, not just from sensation but from the feeling of safety. From knowing, at that moment, that all was well.

ACKNOWLEDGMENTS

As is often said, no book is ever written alone, and this is no exception. My partner and editor, Aurora Foo, was by my side every step of the way in the creation of this book, and to her I have no end of gratitude. Many thanks to Elena Abbott and Issy Waldrom for their encouragement as the book was written. Every author loves a keen beta reader, and Tris Husband was that for us in spades. Also big thanks to May Peterson and Dani Finn for creating a lovely, warm environment for authors to inspire each other. And to Wolffie, thanks for all the encouragement and best of luck with school!

Also, big thanks to Emma Martello for her amazing art for the cover. You can follow her on Bluesky at @gelidspace.bsky.social.

Sophia Turner is a Kiwi trans woman based in Canberra, Australia. She's a programming language designer turned author with a love of all things trans and lesbian. Soph lives with her partner, and they are often seen laughing together over a bowl of ramen.

From The Inside

Taking the Road Barefoot